D1118780

A
SORRY STATE

by the same author

One Hundred Thousand Welcomes
May You Die in Ireland

A
SORRY STATE

Michael Kenyon

David McKay Company, Inc.
Ives Washburn, Inc.
New York

MAY 9 1974

A SORRY STATE

COPYRIGHT © 1974 BY MICHAEL KENYON

All rights reserved, including the right to reproduce
this book, or parts thereof, in any form, except for
the inclusion of brief quotations in a review.

LIBRARY OF CONGRESS CATALOG CARD NUMRER: 74-77480

ISBN 0-679-50463-X

MANUFACTURED IN THE UNITED STATES OF AMERICA

CHAPTER I

'SHOULD WE go through the file, sir?'

'In a while,' said the square grey man, peeling back the seal from a can of Guinness. 'I'm toasting Paddy Byrne, and may he get off with twenty years, or fifteen, because if it wasn't for him being out there, we'd not be up here, and God knows it makes a change.'

The seal parted from the can with an explosive pop, the can tilted, and a black brew like brimstone slurped and curdled into the Perspex tumbler.

'I don't mind telling you,' the grey man said, 'I've the holiday feeling. I'd say I'd even let him off with ten, unless they prove the murders, which they likely won't. Here's to Byrne. Know how much the taxpayer's paying for these tickets, Derry? It is Derry, isn't it?'

'It is.'

'A pretty penny, I'll tell you. A mess of noughts like in the business columns. A queue of noughts.' The square older man sank his upper lip through foam, probing for the brimstone. His jutting eyebrows, parched and grey like grass in a summer drought, tickled the rim of the tumbler. 'Noughts like plates in a shooting-gallery, Derry. Commas like flies. It's on your ticket.'

'You have my ticket, sir.'

'I have?' The older man burrowed in inner pockets of his grey suit.

Holy Mary, he's tight, the younger man realized, and cast a sideways look at his neighbour. The name of the younger man was Maguire. His complexion was an outdoor pink and his eyebrows were unremarkable, but across his upper lip and swooping downward past the corners of his mouth raged a fierce black moustache which from time to time he would placate with caresses from the back of his thumb. Between the eyebrows there now burrowed two vertical frown-lines. Embarrassed, Detective-Sergeant Maguire picked at the foil round the neck of his miniature sherry. Jesus God, he thought, fifteen minutes on the way and the Chief's tight.

He tried to recall if ever he'd heard talk of the Chief being a demon for the booze, but he had not. The Chief's reputation was considerable, and the Sergeant was in awe of it, but it derived from features more eccentric than mere booze. One story was that he dreamed dreams. Might he also be timid of flying, of heights, Maguire wondered, and the booze was like a kind of sedative? But Maguire had met the Super only twice before, and never socially, never in conversations where such snippets might have become revealed. Until an hour ago, when he'd spotted him striding into the VIP lounge, he'd not even known it was going to be the Super. His briefing had been that he'd be travelling with Chief Inspector Connor.

'This one seems to be yours, sir. The other must be mine.'

The older man retrieved the air ticket, examined it, examined a second ticket, dropped the first ticket, and recovered it with sighing and muttering. He passed the second ticket to Maguire.

'We'd have been First Class to London if it hadn't been all booked, so that's saving the taxpayer something,' Maguire said.

Shouted above the roar of four jet engines, the statement was of such phenomenal lack of interest that Maguire, glancing sideways, noticed with relief that the Super had not heard. Detective-Superintendent O'Malley, Chief of the Garda Siochana Central Detective Unit, Dublin Castle, had twisted round in his seat to peer through the window and pronounce an unreluctant farewell, if only for a couple of days or so, to his native city.

He was a hundred miles too late. Even had Dublin Bay been below, which it no longer was, the Aer Lingus jetplane now rode above obliterating rainclouds. O'Malley looked at his watch. Five past noon, Wednesday. He turned again to the oyster-coloured world through the window and inhaled. The abrupt, unexpected flight from routine, the free travel, and the Guinness, elated him. Flying, a passenger was beyond responsibility except for the fastening of seat-belts, extinguishing of cigarettes, and ensuring articles in the overhead lockers were secure.

Easy with the grog, he advised himself. You'll be spreading alarm and despondency among the ranks.

At a time when the rest of Ireland had been striking into cornflakes and Galtee bacon, O'Malley's Wednesday had begun with the Assistant Commissioner thrusting upon him a large Jameson's and news that he, O'Malley, had two hours to pack a bag, find his passport, collect the Byrne file from Chief Inspector Connor, and get his jabs at the airport.

'You'll be needing this where you're going, O'Malley,' the Assistant Commissioner had said. 'Guns, goons, guerrillas, Godfathers, isn't that it? Keep out of all that. You'll come straight back with our man. If we can get him here before his mates slide out of their holes, perhaps this time we'll hold him. *Slainte,* O'Malley, and bring us a coconut.'

Freshly appointed, the Assistant Commissioner was promoting himself as a character. O'Malley, shuddering, had swallowed the second breakfast whiskey, and fled. The escort duty was to have been Connor's, but Mrs Connor, laughing at calendars, had gone suddenly into labour. In Jury's, one minute after opening time, Connor had handed over the Byrne file and an unwanted pint of stout to his pal O'Malley, grumbling as he did so. It wasn't as though this baby'd be the first. It'd be the seventh. But seventh or seventeenth a husband's place was at hand, if possible, so he'd lost a trip to the far side of the world. Only once before, Connor gloomed, had he travelled abroad on duty, expenses paid, and that'd been a day trip to London.

'I've been only twice meself,' countered O'Malley, gulping the parting stout. 'Glasgow both times.'

In the VIP lounge the airport manager had pressed on him a whiskey, and a lesser measure for the villainous-looking Sergeant. 'Sorry we couldn't squeeze you into First,' said the manager, guilty and upset. 'Overbooked time and again. Another quick one?'

'. . . Mr O'Malley?'

O'Malley jolted out of his reverie and turned from the oyster view. Young Sherlock, moustached like a Guatemalan bandit, was nudging his arm. The priest in the aisle seat was inclining forward, regarding him benevolently. Smiling down from the aisle, green and freckled, a hostess was saying something.

'I will, why not? Same again,' O'Malley told her, smiling back. If he'd had children she'd have been of an age to be a daughter. He suppressed an urge to lean across and shake her hand. 'The altitude's dehydrating. Thanks.'

'It's your seat-belt, Mr O'Malley. Would you buckle it up? We're coming in to London.'

On the next leg of the journey O'Malley awoke from the noisiest dream he had ever heard. He was aware that he had not in fact heard anything, for dreams were silent, or at any rate his were, but there'd been a pop group of four once familiar faces and a fifth face which was unmistakably Paddy Byrne, all in squalling unison. Against a battery of lobbed missiles and rioting, the quintet had held their ground, defiant, ducking the missiles, torturing their stereophonic guitars, and baying a slow anthem with lyrics that were largely inaudible through the din.

' "Don' be afraid," ' sang the harmonious group, as though seeking assurance.

The policeman pressed his palms against his ears, yawned, pinched his nose, and cupped his hands again over his ears. His skull sang, his tongue was tasty as an actor's hairpiece. The aircraft was in semi-darkness, and about his head hung an odour of lime air-freshener. O'Malley looked at his neighbour, who was underlining passages in a book.

'What's this then?' Unable to recall the fellow's first name, or his second, he added, 'Sergeant,' and hoped he'd hit on the right rank.

Sergeant Maguire closed the cover of the book so that his chief might see. O'Malley read aloud, *'Islands in Ferment. Asia's Problem Child.'* He nodded. 'Good work. What time is it?'

'Coming up to eleven.'

'Eleven?' O'Malley stared at his watch. His upper arm throbbed from the doctor's pricking and scratching. 'I've five to eight.'

'You've to shift her forward three hours, sir. There was an announcement.'

'Mother of God. What else is happening?'

'There was supper but I didn't like to wake you.'

'We had supper. The duck with the bits of black stuff.'

'That was dinner, sir. The truffles. Supper was lobster. We're over Russia. Another hour we'll be in Tobolsk.'

'Tobolsk is it? We'll have to drink to that,' and intercepting the *Angst* that spread across the Sergeant's face, the older man added, 'Coffee.' He reached up for the call-button.

The BOAC jet swarmed through the night sky. A steward arrived swallowing and flicking meringue from his lips.

'Could you do us a pot of coffee?' O'Malley said. 'And a bottle of champagne.'

He told the Sergeant, 'It's called tapering-off. Don't worry, lad. Get out the file, we'll do our homework.' He stood, stretched, stepped past Maguire, and walked in the wake of the steward.

In the washroom he washed, shaved with an electric razor because it was there, and cleaned his teeth with a wrapped throwaway toothbrush. He wasn't too sure about Maguire: doubtless a good lad, educated, strong on the homework, he'd probably have a filing-box under his bed, but sticky going as a travelling companion. Still and all, to a sprig like Maguire a Superintendent would likely be stickier. O'Malley leaned towards the mirror and stared. In a toneless KGB voice he enunciated, 'Tob-olsk.'

Breathing toothpaste, springy as a pole-vaulter, he walked back along the aisle. He noticed with a pang of nostalgia the absence of nuns and priests. Heathen British, mused O'Malley without rancour, ignoring the innumerable Asiatic faces. He was ready and eager to taper-off. Maguire was too anxious by half, he ought to be doing something about that moustache, not bothering over files. All that was wanted on escort duty was the rogue to be escorted. Maybe the cuffs. For an artist like Paddy Byrne maybe a set of leg-chains too, and one of those iron collars they had in medieval times. And a squadron of guards, and a tank or two in reserve. But files? Summaries and transcripts and photocopies and small print?

Sacred heart, they weren't even half-way yet.

CHAPTER II

THE REFUELLING stop at Tobolsk, a converted military airfield in the empty Soviet heartland, was a disappointment to O'Malley and Maguire. For all they learned of things Russian they as well might have touched down in a field in County Meath. Midnight and cold embraced the jet. At the entrance to a draughty hall they queued for frisking by police. Inside the hall they queued for duty-free loot, and the Sergeant bought a bottle of vodka as a souvenir. O'Malley too asked for vodka, as a gift for Connor, but the lady wrestler manning the cash-drawer scrutinized his Irish banknotes as though they were a challenge to her integrity and rejected them, whereupon O'Malley returned the vodka, and borrowing Bank of England notes from Maguire asked for scotch instead, muttering that he'd burn in hell before he'd support any damned godless profiteering communist vodka industry. Through the windows of the draughty hall twinkled the landing-lights of TWA and JAL jumbos. An Aeroflot Tupolev 144 taxied along an illuminated runway. The BOAC passengers queued to quit the hall and regain their jet.

In the darkened lime-scented tunnel that was the aircraft's one superclass cabin, the Irish policemen tipped back their seats and closed their eyes. As dawn lightened the sky, and the jet hurtled from Soviet into Chinese airspace, the first window-blinds slid up. Watches were moved on another three hours, breakfast arrived, and was cleared. Stewards slid the blinds down, and a cinema screen.

'Should we take a look at the file now, sir?' The voice was eager.

'In a while, Derry. 'Tis a western. We'll give it a spin.'

At the Tunhwang stopover passengers were frisked by guards wearing caps with a red star above the peak. Maguire bought a silk sash for his sister. 'You could've got it half the price in Grafton Street,' O'Malley said, and observing the dismay in the Sergeant's eyes regretted having spoken. Through a gap between the airport buildings could be seen a featureless plain, and on the horizon a ridge of mountains. Maguire informed that if the direction were south-east the hills could be Inner Mongolia.

Fatigued, sated with food and miles, the BOAC passengers filed back aboard. With the five-course lunch the Superintendent called for a bottle of claret and resumed his tapering-off, ignoring most of the courses but emitting a sigh with each sip of wine. Afterwards he flipped through the Sergeant's *Islands in Ferment*, then dozed, then prised off his shoes and slept deeply while Maguire, recovering his book, continued the underlining. At Hong Kong the jet refuelled for Sydney, and the policemen collected their modest baggage and waited three hours for their PAL flight across the South China Sea. White-shirted students, refugees from the tenements of neighbouring streets, sat along the upholstered benches with heads bowed over textbooks.

'Watches on another hour, sir,' Sergeant Maguire advised. The policemen fastened their seat-belts, and when the plane was airborne Maguire went to the magazine rack and returned with a Manila newspaper. The Filipino hostess who floated through First Class dispensing menus and tenderness was the most beautiful girl ever seen by either man.

'What's this meal then, Derry?' O'Malley said.

'Sort of early dinner, sir. Or late lunch.' The Sergeant opened his menu and read aloud. 'Fresh seafood cocktail, *potage au cresson*, or *potage de poisson, rôti de bœuf Luzon*, with lima beans – '

'We'll skip it,' said O'Malley.

He could not have explained to Maguire, because he did not know himself, why the carnival spirit which had embarked with him at Dublin and buoyed him up through more than a day and a night, so suddenly had deserted him. Neither was there anything to be won by remarking to the Sergeant that which was nothing more than a foreboding. The presentiment of disorder, even chaos ahead, burrowed like a grub in his mind, but he did not try to shrug it out of existence merely because it had no rational basis. All his years the Superintendent had been a perplexed believer in there being more things in heaven and earth.

'Get out the file,' he said.

'Patrick Colman Byrne,' Maguire said, reading from the file. He inclined towards his Chief and raised his voice above the engine-roar. 'Born Dublin, Nineteen –'

'Keep your voice down.'

'Sir.'

Sergeant Maguire was also suffering in his mind, but the trouble seemed physical rather than mental. The assembling of his thoughts had become a struggle. His brain had grown listless, and concentrate as he might, thoughts flowed with the celerity of hardening cement. What doubled his suffering and left him feeling cross was the fact that the Super, for the first time on the trip, was alert. He, Maguire, had been cautious with the alcohol, yet the Chief, who out of Dublin had been a discredit to the force, now was as sharp as a fishwife's tongue. Admittedly he'd eaten more than the Super, after all it was the gourmet stuff and all free, he'd not missed a meal until now, or a course in a meal, sometimes in fact asking for seconds, especially of the puddings. He'd not slept so much as the Super either. Now he thought of it, and thinking of it Maguire began to feel sorry for himself, the Super had slept a great deal, and while he'd slept, he, the team's number two, had been doing the work, learning up about these Philippine Islands, ethnic variety and national resources and the

like, and giving consideration to the criminal Byrne.
Apart from one cramped nap he'd not slept at all. He'd
been too wound up. How could the Super not be wound
up with all this gallivanting across the world at the taxpayer's expense and the business of bringing back to
Dublin a wild animal like Byrne?

Was it a question of experience? Had the Chief
drugged himself to sleep with tablets because of the
heights? Maguire was convinced the Super's trouble had
been the heights. He felt sorrow for his own relative
inexperience. In relation, that was, to the experience of
Superintendents. God, but his mind was dopey.

'Go on then, lad.'

'Patrick Colman Byrne, born Dublin, Nineteen thirty-
six – '

'We had that,' O'Malley said.

'Youngest of four brothers, James, Joseph – '

'We don't want the brothers.'

'Father, Brendan Byrne, bench-hand, no record.'
Maguire swallowed, persecuted, frustration mingling
with dopeyness. 'Mother, Winifred Byrne, seventeen cases
shoplifting, sundry drunk and disorderly, deceased Nineteen fifty-one.' He wished the trip were over and he
were back in Dublin. Self-pity, product of self-indulg-
ence and the Super's brusqueness, had set up a prickling
sensation in his eyes. 'Attended Christian Brothers'
School, Mayo Road, Rathmines. School reports – '

'We don't want any of that. What about the singing?'

'Sir?'

'Get to the singing. 'Fifty-nine or 'Sixty. Thereabouts.
The Young Farmers, Kilkenny.'

Sergeant Maguire turned pages. He'd have liked to
have known why the Super wanted to get to anything

since he knew it all already, the ox. 'July eighteenth,' he read, 'Kilkenny branch Young Farmers' Association dinner-dance, Blessed Oliver Plunket Hall.'

'That's it.'

'Concussed two guards. Stage wrecked, a half-dozen Young Farmers hospitalized. Byrne got three months in the Joy.'

'That was the start,' O'Malley said. 'Wonder what he'd have been singing.'

'Doesn't say.'

' 'Course it doesn't say. Probably doesn't say what was in the sandwiches either. Was it the ballads, *Mother Machree*, or the pops?'

'Sir?'

'Which?'

'Couldn't say.'

He's sulking, O'Malley realized. 'Go on then,' he said. 'Next offence.'

'New York as you'll remember where he emigrated to further his singing career after a degree of passport jiggery-pokery calling himself Paddy Brennan as you're aware, sir.'

I'm going to have to tread on this gouger, O'Malley told himself.

'Nine months, assaulting a traffic cop,' read Maguire.

'Broke his jaw?'

'In three places. Five years for armed robbery, San Quentin. Released after two. Three in Denver for robbery and malicious wounding with a barrel divider.'

'Whatever that is.'

'A barrel divider's what you – '

'Wait. We'll have a glass of champagne.' He reached for the call-button. 'It's all on the ticket, lad, and the return trip's going to be abstemious. Though it might be a notion, I don't know what your thoughts'd be on this, to get Byrne drunk. Drunk and unconscious.'

'If you think it's a good idea.'

What's upset the feller, O'Malley wondered. He gazed through the window at wisps of cloud, and the crawling sea forty thousand feet below.

It wasn't such a cracked idea either, having Byrne flutered. A case like Byrne might take some handling. These new lads with their exam certificates and quick promotion, they didn't know. The Byrnes of the world weren't after padding along quietly with a yes sir, no sir, three bags full sir.

CHAPTER III

SWALLOWING CHAMPAGNE like a wedding-guest, Superintendent O'Malley tried not to let his mind wander too haphazardly while the Sergeant progressed through the file.

Byrne deported from the States and back in Ireland, capering with the Provisionals; Byrne falling foul of the Provisionals, and his vendetta with them; Byrne the renegade, offering his services to the British army in the North, and snubbed; Byrne taken by the Irish army following a flurry of futile, indiscriminate killings and bombings in the Fermanagh border area; Byrne lighting out from the Curragh military camp while awaiting trial, and leaving behind a dead corporal, several maimed, and twenty dynamited tons of rubble. There were gaps in the quotes reaching O'Malley's ears because his thoughts strayed to ballad-singing, of which he was no devotee, and to fishing, of which he was, and to the Curragh, where the previous Saturday he'd lost five sheets on the colt Bonus, trained by McGrath and tipped by that smart-alec newcomer on the *Press*. The Sergeant's voice hummed on, a bee-swarm of sound, expressionless as a child reading to its teacher. Once during a gap in which O'Malley realized that his thoughts were not wandering but waiting, expectant, for the next file revelation, he turned and found the Sergeant staring fixedly at nothing on the back of the seat in front of him.

'All right, Derry?'

'What?'

'Feeling all right?'

'I am of course.' The Sergeant became active with a court record filed in Denver, Colorado, fidgeting through papers.

'Is it the height?'

'Height of what?'

'Up here. There are some flying doesn't suit. It'll be the height, lad. Nothing to be ashamed of.'

' 'Tis not the height. I'm grand.'

O'Malley shrugged, sipped.

'I like the height,' insisted Maguire, petulant, and bowing his head towards the papers he began to intone a state attorney's instruction to the jury.

The file was bulky, not because Byrne's track record was particularly long or heavily documented, indeed a chasm separated the Curragh escape from present times, a three-year vacuum into which Byrne had dropped comprehensively from sight; but because Willie Connor had assembled it with zeal, concerning himself with the case beyond the requirements of normal procedure. Not only did the buff folder hold the routine copies of charge-sheets, police photographs, transcripts of trials, and prison governors' reports, but there were unnecessary press cuttings and shiny dinner-jacketed publicity photos dating from the singing days. There was a wedge of material on the unsolved border murders, a ripe selection from the embarrassed minutes of committees which had leaped into session after the Curragh escape, and most recently, after a three-year blank, the Manila material.

'I'll borrow that,' said O'Malley, and took from the Sergeant the brochures and stapled newspaper cuttings relating to the Philippines.

He had glanced through them in the car to Dublin Airport but absorbed nothing. Slouched in his cushioned seat, O'Malley now read with care, while up and down the aisle stewards and the radiant hostess served *rôti de bœuf Luzon*, and in the adjacent seat unfed Maguire sulked over his Manila newsaper.

The Manila material was thin because until four days ago, when the Philippines Constabulary had sent word to Dublin that they were holding a man named Burke, who might be a man listed by the Interpol clearing-house as Byrne, the same who in the USA had called himself Brennan, and would Dublin like to send someone to remove him, there had been never a hint that Byrne was in the Philippines rather than in Belfast, or the Kerry hills, or Pittsburgh, or Greenland. The newspaper clippings included an unsettling paragraph about an air crash on the Philippines island of Cebu, and cursory stories about a trade agreement, a typhoon, the disquali-fication of Miss Philippines from the Miss Universe con-test on being found to be fourteen years old, the growing

drug menace in Manila, and a jungle search for another
nest of geriatric Japanese soldiers in hiding since the
Second World War. The tourist brochures painted panchromatic pictures of lagoons, pearl divers, rice terraces
three thousand years old, unruffled wood-carvers, and
neon-lit nite-life.

*Mahubay — or Welcome to the Philippines! Seven
thousand Tropical Isles to which You will Lose Your
Heart! Spiced with the Glamor of Old Spain! Thrill to
Languorous Days and Exotic Nights!*

Was that, mused O'Malley, perusing the livid publicity, what Paddy Byrne had been up to the past year
or two, thrilling in the Philippines? Where'd the man
found the loot for languorous days and exotic nights?

A possible answer faced him out of the clipped column, three months old, from *Time*. Two years previously, it appeared, the Aussie airline Qantas, jumpy
about upheavals in the Philippines, had jettisoned Manila
from its list of scheduled ports. Now, which was to say
three months ago, JAL was planning to defect. The upheavals, reported *Time*, were not so much geological,
though earthquakes occurred from time to time, as political. Violence was endemic, much of it mere gangster-
ism, but the guerrillas who in the New Year had fought
their way to the suburbs of Manila before being turned
back were Maoists, descendants of the Huk rebels of
the 'fifties, and far from being crushed were regrouping
with increased support from the peasants. The Yankee
guerrilla leader Ewart Hart had promised that Manila
would be taken and the government and all its running-
dog lackeys executed within the year. Senator Alvaro
Cruz, Liberal Party opposition leader, was under house
arrest. Martial law had been reintroduced, the President

had been seen only once since the New Year, and democracy, not for the first time in this restless republic, was imperilled. Corruption, enthused the *Time* reporter, was rife, and the gun and the bolo were the solution to every dispute. The newly built and rebuilt International Airport had been sabotaged three times since the early 'seventies, and on two occasions undisclosed quantities of arms and ammunition had been stolen during raids on the American airbase at Clark Airfield. In the ore-and-timber-rich island of Mindanao, its placid waters the cemetery of sunken galleons and the bleached bones of conquistadores (I'd bleach the bones of this reporter feller for a start, O'Malley thought), speculators and commercial interests were decimating the stone-age tribes. In Manila, drugs, smuggling and mayhem had escalated beyond the control of an underpaid, largely illiterate police force. The previous week in a shoot-out in the lobby of the sumptuous Intercontinental Hotel, a desk clerk had been wounded, a tourist killed. The tourist, 57-year-old Mrs Louisa Paul of Seattle, had come from the manicurist and was standing by No. 7 elevator . . .

And so on, with fervour and adjectives. Connor had ringed the references to smuggling, and the raid on Clark Airbase, and in the margin written, *PB – Mahogany*.

Was the smuggling of stolen arms, pondered O'Malley, the source of the cash which Byrne-Burke-Brennan had grabbed for his languorous days and exotic nights, if languor and exoticism was what he was up to? Of three separate consignments of Philippines mahogany which had arrived by freighter in Ireland over the past year, only the last had been unbound, picked apart and peered into by a customs pair in whom duty had warred

with boredom. Startled, the customs men had peered
through timbers into a cache of assorted automatic rifles,
machine-guns, grenades, and boxes of ammunition.

Someone else can puzzle over that, O'Malley told
himself. One job at a time. Mine's gathering Byrne and
keeping him from hi-jacking the plane on the trip home.
Passing the Manila material back to the Sergeant, he
said :

'What's a bolo?'

Sergeant Maguire remained silent, deafly gazing at
the newspaper on his lap but not, in O'Malley's opinion,
seeing it. Knocked out by the height and pressure and
all, judged the Superintendent. Not the lad's fault. All
the same it'd have to have a line in the report. O'Malley
did not bother to repeat the question. The newspaper
headline read, SENATOR CRUZ SLAMS NACION-
ALISTAS, and further down the page, CALOOCAN
WIDOW REUNITED WITH RUNAWAY DAUGH-
TER, and across the page, FAMILY OF FIVE BE-
HEADED. He caught the blur of a passing radiance,
and beckoned.

'Could you manage another drop of the champagne,
would y' say?' he said.

The hostess smiled like the Song of Solomon, and
when she returned with napkin-swaddled bottle the
Superintendent said by way of conversation, there being
no conversation with Sergeant Maguire, 'You've the
martial law in Manila?'

'Oh no.'

'Oh?' He watched her set down a doily, and on the
doily a glass. 'It's been lifted?'

'Oh yes. I guess so.' The smile persisted, a rictus acquired at hostess school. She would wear it always,

O'Malley supposed : tying her shoelaces, asleep, running for buses. 'Curfew maybe,' she said, pouring. 'Your first visit?'

'It is.'

'Well fine. Welcome. You'll have a nice time.' The amber wine fizzed and foamed in the glass. 'You are staying long?'

'Only tonight,' said O'Malley, and the foreboding crawled back, bringing an image of Ewart Hart, bearded like Guevara, leading his guerrillas into burning, curfew-empty Manila.

'But that's terrible.' Terrible though it was, the smile held, indestructible. 'You can see nothing in a night.'

'It's cruel, no mistake.'

'You'll have a wonderful time,' she said illogically, and with the napkin caught the drip from the bottle.

After she had departed, O'Malley said to the Sergeant, 'Hear that? Curfew. Bed by ten sharp tonight.'

But Maguire was as though already there, deaf and marble-eyed, folding and refolding the newspaper with the heavy purposeless movements of an automaton.

At five in the afternoon the PAL airliner taxied to a halt on its home ground. The Irish policemen and a slow queue of passengers stepped out into the kitchen heat. To the left, beyond the tarmac and a belt of undistinguished green, rose the shell of the airport building, roofless, windowless, its steel and concrete walls charred by fire, brambles disfiguring the once hopeful exits and entrances. Sabotaged first during the second term of President Marcos, partially rebuilt, then sabotaged a second and third time, as though deemed the ideal practice ground for trainees, it stood out against the sky

like a film set, a gaunt blackened structure bidding its
own bizarre *Mabuhay* to arriving passengers. On the
tarmac at the base of the jetplane's steps stood four or
five routine officials: ground staff, the coach drivers,
two policemen.

'Don't see any reception committee,' O'Malley murmured. 'You sure this is Manila?'

'Sir?' Maguire said.

They reached the ground, and to the nearest policeman O'Malley said, 'My name's O'Malley,' and
watched for the sign of recognition. The sign did not
appear. The policeman waved towards the waiting
coaches.

'Superintendent O'Malley,' endeavoured O'Malley.
'From Dublin. Ireland.'

In the coach O'Malley watched through the window
as though half expecting to spot Byrne, manacled and
guarded, awaiting deportation. He recalled the Assistant
Commissioner's briefing.

'It's a bit tricky because we've no extradition treaty
with the Philippines,' the AC had said, and he had gestured with the Jameson's bottle. 'They don't seem to have
an extradition treaty with anyone. But we're invited so
there shouldn't be any problem. You'll have to spend
Thursday night. Friday morning they put our boy on a
flight to Hong Kong. You'll be on the same flight and
that's where you take over. Once in Hong Kong we're all
right. All clear with the Home Office. Only forty minutes before your flight to London. Something like that.
Connor'll fill you in. You'll be back in Dublin Saturday
evening.'

The arrivals building was a shack which at one time
had been considered temporary. The makeshift count-

ers had taken root. There were benches with lounging customs officials, a gloomy bar, a shop stocked with beads and carved water-buffalo, exhausted travellers, porters, hire-car representatives with badges, and policemen standing idly with scatter-guns, unobtrusively remote from the activity. Apart from one or two overdressed arrivals such as the passengers O'Malley and Maguire, men wore shirt-sleeves, women showed brown arms bare to the shoulder. In tired silence passports were stamped. The dominant noise was the whirring of an antique air-conditioning unit.

'D'you see a phone?' O'Malley said.

His eyes held on a man in khaki uniform and peaked cap who had entered fast through a door and was heading towards the mob off the PAL flight, searching their faces. He came forward. His patent-leather shoes were small and pointed, his tailored trousers tighter than those of a youth on the prowl. He had the confident air of a silent-screen idol accomplishing, successfully, the transition from young lover to middle-aged rake.

'Superintendent O'Malley?'

'That's right.'

'Rodrigo.' He removed the cap to reveal patent-leather hair, and extended his hand. 'Your first impression of our Manila police is not going to be high. I was told of your arrival only half an hour ago.'

'We're just in. This is Sergeant Maguire.'

'Sergeant,' Rodrigo said, shaking Maguire's hand, and his smile showed teeth so white that they might have been capped only that morning by the studio's dental surgeon. 'My car's outside.'

But he made no move. The air-conditioning unit gave a muffled clatter and fell silent. Looking from Maguire to O'Malley, and starting to fan himself with the khaki cap, Rodrigo said, 'Your second impression will be lower than your first.'

'You've lost Byrne,' O'Malley said.

'Ah?' The cap stalled, the black Filipino eyes widened in admiration. 'But only at noon. How can you have known?'

CHAPTER IV

THE AIR-CONDITIONING in the Buick with the domed roof-light and emblazoned Manila Police insignia was noiseless and cool. The driver wore a khaki short-sleeved shirt, open at the neck, adorned with cloth badges on the shoulders, and chrome badges on the epaulettes and over the left breast pocket. The peak of his flat cap was drawn low over his eyes like a blind. He eased the car into the traffic on the airport road, holding to the tail of a police car in front, and accelerated behind the leading police car along the fast lane.

In the back seat Maguire meditated on the roominess of the back seat, and come to that, of the front seat. His Chief sat next to him, and in the far corner was the Rodrigo ponce, but there were gaps enough for a fourth, even for a willowy fifth if the Super hadn't taken space enough for two. With the stateliness of a new dawn a second thought filtered through to Maguire: that numberless as were the times he'd seen cars of this class on the TV, this was the first occasion he'd sat in one. If he'd been a top foreign cop with use of a car, he thought, this'd be the car he'd have had, with a hard man to drive it, and the siren screaming to let people know the law

was on its way. Which switch, he wondered, leaning
forward and peering, would be the siren? God, there was
a mess of tackle. Colonel Rodrigo was saying:

'He was in Camp Crame. That's the Philippines Constabulary. Quezon City, not Manila.' The accent was
American, the delivery quick and throwaway. 'Always
the same. No liaison, just bickering, passing the buck. If
we'd had him in the first place, I promise you we would
have held him.'

'Did he, that's to say,' said O'Malley, 'was anyone
hurt?'

'He was sprung. He walked out in police uniform and
was driven away. There was no one to hurt.'

'Well, thanks be to God.'

'Thanks be to some I could name. It'd be a pleasure to
see them shipped out to sea and dropped quietly over-
board. Now they pass it to us, to me, this afternoon. They
wash their hands. I am sorry, believe me.' The Colonel
lit a cigarillo. There were rings on his fingers: gold
signet, a plain silver band, a milky pearl. 'What do you
do now?'

'Tell Dublin.'

'They are going to be delighted.' A jet of smoke issued
from the Colonel's lips. 'You prefer beaches or casinos,
Mr O'Malley? Our best casino reopened last week. You
fancy your chances, go tonight, tomorrow it could be
closed down again. For your information I will tell you.
Tomorrow it will be closed down again.'

'The Huns are at the gates?'

'Huns?'

'Huns, Vandals. Maoists. What's his name, Ewart
Hart?'

'I thought you said Huks. They have been at the gates

quite a while, and inside the gates, only they're not Huks any more. Hart joined them when he deserted at Corregidor. Then they were Huks. Now they're Maoists. First the Maoist New People's Army, now the Free Maoist Army of Liberation. The new guerrilla generation. The post-Huks. It is not what they call themselves bothers me, it is how straight they shoot.'

Corregidor. There, ruminated O'Malley, was a name to conjure with. But how conjure? What exactly and where was Corregidor? O'Malley raked his memory, resenting his ignorance. All that emerged was an image of John Wayne in steel helmet, storming the heights. The Buick, following the first police car, turned left off Quirino Avenue and raced along the right-hand lane towards a blood-orange sun. The landscape was flat, uninspired, spiked with billboards.

'And where they are getting,' Rodrigo said, 'what they shoot with.'

'That can't be a problem,' said a voice. 'You've a million firearms in private possession, twenty times as many as all your army and police've got, and that was back in seventy-three.'

The two senior policemen turned their heads and looked at Maguire. Maguire looked away, up at the ceiling, then at his knees. He attacked his moustache with his thumb.

'*Islands in Ferment*,' he mumbled.

Nodding, regarding the Sergeant with too much respect to be sincere, Rodrigo said, 'I'd put the figure closer to a million and a half. What your, ah, source perhaps does not say, Sergeant, is that most of these firearms are museum-pieces. Relics from the war. The guns the guerrillas are getting are semi-automatic, Lee-Enfield carbines, the M-Six.' He inhaled from the cigarillo, smiled whitely, and holding his breath allowed the smoke to sidle upwards from his nostrils. 'All new. American.'

'There were four cases of M-Sixes in the mahogany,' Maguire said, and winced as his Chief's elbow prodded his ribs.

'Look at that sky, lad,' O'Malley said. 'Didja ever see such a sight?'

Maguire looked and silently agreed that probably he'd never seen such an overwhelming sunset, but he was downcast, unsure of the reason for the prod. The Colonel said :

'If it's agreeable to you, O'Malley, I suggest we go first to headquarters. You can phone. My office is yours. And I'd like you to see a letter from Washington. The Americans have been very upset. They have invested in this country and rebellion does not help. At the same time they cannot be seen to be interfering. Now at least they know, they have confirmed, the M-Sixes smuggled into your country, and those the guerrillas are getting, are from the same source.'

'They know more than I do,' O'Malley said.

'They need to. The source is their own Clark Airbase.'

'They should look into that.'

'They're looking into a number of things. For instance, you can't blame them for pulling in your Mr Burke.'

'Byrne. If it's all the same, I'll think of him as Byrne. Did they talk to him at all?'

'I am told an officer tried, from the airbase, and someone from their Embassy.'

'What about the who is it, whoever had him, your constabulary? I'd like to take back their report.'

'There is no report. I have inquired. And if we get

one, I warn you, it will be worthless.'

'I see.'

'I am not sure that you do. Truthfully, how much would you say you know about this country? Would it fill the back of an envelope?'

O'Malley looked at the Colonel, who twisted his head so that the jet of exhaled smoke billowed against the window. The Superintendent looked the other way, past Maguire, towards the sunset. The armoured ships in Manila Bay glowed pink from the sun's dying light.

'Might,' O'Malley said, 'if I spread it around a bit.'

'Europeans, not maybe so much in Spain, but the rest of you, you have to reach for an atlas,' Rodrigo said. 'We are the last undiscovered country. I read your newspapers sometimes. We do not rate a mention, except at election times when your leader writers bring out their brightest sneers. You, Ireland, you haven't even an embassy here. Yet we are nearly fifty million people, all but a few of us Catholics. Right, embassies cost money. But you see? No information, no interest. It's inevitable you should be innocent. So I must explain.' The Colonel wound down the window and threw out the cigarillo. The hot outside air gusted into the Buick. 'This Burke, or Byrne, is free – that is not the word, he cost someone a great deal – he is loose because here, O'Malley, everything is for sale, and someone has paid for him to be set loose.'

O'Malley grunted and waited. He had crossed his legs and sunk deeper into the upholstery in anticipation of the explanation. Apparently the explanation was over.

'I see,' he said, and hurriedly, 'That's to say.' But as nothing useful came to mind he remained silent. The silence grew uncomfortable. 'Well, money talks,' he said.

'Whoever has the kind of money that talked Byrne out of Camp Crame has friends,' said Rodrigo. 'Whether they're the rebels or street gangsters or the Constabulary Commander or the President himself. Let me be truthful. I shall do my best to get Byrne back for you. But I am not optimistic. I am sorry. I fear you have had a wasted journey.'

The Buick flung itself soundlessly along the coast road, northward towards the lights of the city. Flat-roofed factories, Coca-Cola hoardings, and bursts of crowded, rotting dwellings of bamboo and thatch sped past on the right. To the left, across the bay, the sunset stretched like a bloody gash above the black humps of Corregidor and Bataan.

'If your office is anywhere close to the Hilton we'll drop off the Sergeant,' O'Malley said.

'Practically next door.'

'I think I'll come along, sir,' said Maguire, 'if that's all right.'

'You'll get some sleep, lad,' O'Malley said. 'The travel fatigue's nothing to be ashamed of.'

CHAPTER V

MAGUIRE, sleepless in pyjamas, lay in the dark with his eyes open. He felt more cross than ashamed, and intrigued more than anything.

It was the travel fatigue right enough. He'd heard of it. The ailment the tycoons caught when they dashed from here to yonder, five miles up, moving their watches this way and that like timekeepers at a sports day. It had to be the travel fatigue because all he was good for was sleep, but he wasn't sleeping. Two hours of straining to tip into the abyss and he was as destroyed as when he'd started and twice as wakeful. Hadn't he always been a stupendous sleeper till now? Out to the world the moment he hit the pit? No supper either, he'd been dropped by the brass and straight to bed. But for all the use he might as well have been up and about, achieving things. Question was, would a swallow from the complimentary bottle of rum on the dressing-table put him out or get him excited?

Second question was, was it complimentary? How'd he know it wouldn't be scribbled on the bill the instant he popped the bung out? And what'd the accounts fellas in Dublin say to that? The Super wouldn't care, he'd be drinking his soon as he caught sight of it, no mistake, but what about when the bills got back to the Castle? There'd be ructions when they turned up the item, *Sergeant Maguire, One bottle rum,* 40 *pesos.*

There were Cokes in the fridge. Rum-and-Coke, that might be the ticket, he'd heard of rum-and-Coke. *Sergeant Maguire, One bottle rum, One Coca-Cola,* 60 *pesos.* Maybe 160 pesos. You never knew with these fancy hotels.

If the rum had been doctored of course it might put him out for good and ever. He'd not trust anyone in this city. Manila, what he'd glimpsed of it, was spooky. All those khaki guns at the airport, and guards in blue down in the lobby, with more guns, he'd spotted 'em. Heat, spookiness, rum. Byrne's pals, the one the Rodrigo character had mentioned, they'd have been able to raise a quid if it was a matter of being shut of a couple of interloping gardai. Must warn the Super about the rum,

Maguire thought.

He did not move. If the Super was already back he'd have drunk the rum and it'd be too late. Mother of God, but that'd be a sensation in the canteen. O'Malley the Dream, deceased from rum and spooks at the fag end of the world. Couldn't he just hear the excitement and slopped tea and rumours of promotion for someone? All Sergeant Maguire could in fact hear, in his mind's ear, was the withering silence that would follow his advice, 'Sir, don't drink the rum.' Choosing between the Super poisoned and the Super contemptuous would take thinking about.

Before he could think about it, a tingling as from a minor electric shock passed through the Sergeant's body, and he lay tense, sensing with his flesh, muscle and nerve-endings a presence under the bed.

Hearing nothing, but aware of company and a gathering clamminess of the skin, he reached out with his left arm, walking his fingers through darkness in search of the light switch on the bedside console. His elbow nudged something on the console which answered with a scraping sound. At the same moment the telephone shrilled. Maguire jerked upright in bed. His forearm knocked to the carpet an ashtray or fruit basket or Gideon Bible, something that fell with a thud. He found the switch, fumbled, and turned on the radio.

'Cosmetics, trophies, bath scales and all modern appliances,' announced the radio. 'For the lowest prices in town, visit the Anson Emporium at four thirty-seven Juan Luna Street.'

'Don't move now!' Maguire cried, and discovering a neighbouring switch he introduced to a limited area above the bed a pink, romantic glow. He swung out of bed, bounded across the carpet, grasped the foot of the bed, and rejecting as too complicated the possibility that he might be about to pull the wall down, tugged. 'Right so!' he called out above the radio and ringing telephone, and the tugged bed glided so swiftly across the carpet that he had to scurry backwards to avoid being run over. Under the bed and all around, pink in the sensuous lighting, was bare space.

'What animal possesses the largest eyes in the world?' the radio inquired. 'Answer, folks – the great blue whale, whose eyeball is five inches in diameter.'

'Hullo,' Maguire said into the phone. 'Yes?'

He was breathless and sweating. The unkempt bed stood askew in the centre of the room. Spreadeagled by his bare foot lay the leather-bound volume of laundry prices, restaurants, arcade shopping services.

'Hullo,' he repeated.

There came the click. After repeating his greeting a third time, and a fourth, Maguire replaced the phone. The radio had embarked on an Ozark lament with banjo accompaniment. Accompanying the banjo were chime bells and a whining voice.

> He stumbled on in Daddy's wake
> No water for his thirst to slake

Only after the chimes had rung several changes did Maguire realize that they issued not from the Ozarks but from the door. Skirting the bed, he trod with dozy caution past the writing-desk, the television, the ice-box, the clothes closet, and the wardrobe. At the door he listened, and said:

'Who is it?'

'Me,' said O'Malley, muffled through the woodwork. On Maguire's side, shiny and cold against his cheek, was

posted in minuscule print a notice about fire regulations.
The muffled voice said, 'Derry?'

'Yes?'

'You all right?'

'Grand. That you, sir?'

'It is. Are y'awake, then?'

'I am.'

'Who's singing?'

''Tis the wireless.'

'Have you a woman in there?'

'I have not.' In spite of his certainty the Sergeant
turned his head and peered into the dusty pink of the
room. He turned back, mouth to the fire regulations.
'There's me only. I'm alone all evening.'

'Then for the love of God will y'hold your jabber and
let me in?'

The Sergeant unlocked the door. His Chief strode in
scowling, parked his suitcase on the floor, himself in an
armchair, and eyed the askew bed. Sergeant Maguire
locked the door. He was troubled as to how he might be
able to slide the bed back into place surreptitiously, without the Super noticing, or whether he should leave it be,
pretending that was how he'd found it, the method the
Filipinos had of arranging hotel rooms. He was relieved
the management had provided a second armchair. The
thought of receiving the Super from a sitting position in
bed lacked appeal. He said :

'Did you get Dublin, sir?'

'I did not. Two hours' delay. Would you turn that
noise off?' When the radio was silenced, O'Malley said,
'Have you no more light? 'Tis like a brothel.'

Maguire found more light, a blinding effulgence that
leaped into the room from undiscovered sources. He

stayed by the switches where he might be on hand for further requests.

'Byrne was arrested by accident,' O'Malley said. 'That's to say he wasn't arrested by accident, it was an accident he was arrested. What I'm sayin' is.' He sighed and pulled a notebook from his pocket. 'That was a long trip, Derry. Did you sleep?'

'Not yet.'

'Likely it takes a day or two. You should've brought some pills.'

'What about the letter, sir?'

'What letter's that?'

'From Washington. About the guns.'

'Waste of breath, lists and that, gripping stuff for a gunsmith. What I was saying is Colonel Rodrigo says Byrne was drinking with this rebel fella, Hart, and five of his lieutenants.' He turned a page of the notebook. 'A bar some place called Pasay City. The Miami Club, Pasay City. It's a suburb.' From another pocket the Superintendent drew a map. 'He gave me a map.'

'Are we staying, then?'

'Seems Hart's getting bold,' said O'Malley, opening the map. 'It's not the first time he's been spotted in Manila the last month or two, but it was the first time the police got there before he vanished off. There was a heap of shooting. Three dead. Hart and one of his cronies skedaddle, the other two and our Paddy boy get hauled off to this Camp Crame. They've been shot, the other two. Don't ask why they didn't shoot Byrne while they were about it. I've already asked.'

'You don't just shoot people.'

'Well now. You don't, and I don't, though I'd say there's been a time or two I've had it in mind.' O'Malley pushed the notebook into a jacket pocket; the map, an unwieldy sheet of a myriad colours criss-crossed by black routes, overhung his lap. 'Here they've a bit of a war going on, don't y'see. But the rule is you only shoot your own, you don't shoot an Irishman, and you particularly don't shoot him when he's reckoned to have a pal or two among the Yanks. Like Byrne. Makes the tourists shy. This Colonel Rodrigo says it was the President himself said to hold their fire, he thinks.'

'Cold feet.'

'Put your slippers on. Did you not bring slippers?' The Superintendent met with a frown the vacant stare directed at him by his assistant, and said, 'What?'

'What?' Maguire said.

O'Malley shook his head, then bowed it over the map. 'That's Pasay City, we must have driven through it.' He stabbed with a finger. 'I'm taking a look. Might as well go through the motions. If you're not sleeping, come along.'

'Now?'

'You could get some clothes on first. You'll look a case going visiting in pyjamas and that moustache.'

'There's a bottle of rum, sir,' said Maguire. He was bitterly aware that cowardice would prompt him to warn the Super in time. 'If you're eager for a drink.'

'I am not eager for a drink, Sergeant. I'm trying to justify those plane tickets. You think we should sit and look at the wall?'

'Sir.' Maguire swallowed. He had one ace to play. 'Won't you miss your call to Dublin if we go stravaiging off to clubs and places?'

'Cancelled it. Sent a cable. Jump to it, lad. The Colonel's waiting.'

'That pimp.' Maguire, beaten, rustled round the bed in search of shed clothing. 'Is he coming?'

'He sorta insisted. Anyway, it'll save us the taxi fare. And incidentally, lad, a little respect. Colonel Rodrigo, if y'don't mind.' The Superintendent was growing angry over his failure to find the correct folds into which to refold the map. He twisted the sheet about and started punching at it, slapping it on his knees, and creating new ill-tempered folds that had not been there before. 'He's not a pimp either. He's Chief of Police. And if y'ask me, a worried one.'

CHAPTER VI

THE FRAMED notice on the wall inside the entrance to the Miami Club wore the dingy irrelevant air of such close-printed regulations and bye-laws everywhere: as unobserved a fixture as the light-fittings, unread, and due to the unlit corner which the proprietor had managed to find for it, virtually unreadable.

> *Pursuant to Ordinance No. 3820, possessors of firearms and other dangerous weapons not authorized as security guards and other special services are requested to deposit their weapons here.*

O'Malley, Maguire and the Colonel's driver followed the Colonel down steps, through a curtain, and into an umbrageous cellar where someone somewhere was playing a piano. The grinning, flowery-shirted teenager who

stepped forward in greeting did not request the Colonel
to deposit the pistol he carried on his hip, but grinned
at the badges of rank, and in the same fluid movement
which had brought him out of the dark stepped back into
it again, still grinning. The Colonel led past booths and
empty tables towards the bar. The driver, dropping
back and seating himself at a table near the curtained
entrance, snapped his fingers in the direction of the
shadows which had swallowed the teenager.

'You should try a *tuba*,' the Colonel said, placing his
cap on the bar. 'You may hate it but you should try it.
It is very Filipino, and like the Filipinos, a little fiery.'

'Grand,' said O'Malley. A gust of pomade reached
him from the Colonel's hair. Colonel Rodrigo had crossed
his legs on the tall bar-stool and was smiling with immense suavity, consciously contradicting, O'Malley believed, the point tht Filipinos were fiery. 'This where
they sat, at the bar?' O'Malley said.

'Possibly. I have never been before.' The liquorice eyebrows lifted towards Maguire. 'Sergeant?'

'I'll try the *tuba*, sir, thanks.'

'Two *tubas*,' the Colonel told the boy in the white
jacket behind the bar, 'and a *gaseosa*, and tell me, where
did Hart sit Saturday night?'

'First and second booths,' the boy said, pointing, and
swung from behind the bar. Beckoning, turning to be
sure he was being followed, he approached the deserted
booths and struck a match. 'See? And here?' Position-
ing the flame, he placed a finger beside holes in the
woodwork. 'The big one with the sunglasses, señor,
killed right here. One cop shot three, four times.' He held
up four fingers. 'The other at the bar. See.'

The barman scampered back to the bar and struck a

new match. The stained boarding was holed and ravaged as by some monstrous beetle. O'Malley, his eyes growing used to the dark, spotted the pianist against the far wall, beyond the bar, fingering out mood-music to an absentee clientèle. Mood-music to get depressed to, O'Malley thought. In the Miami Club were only two or three customers. One, a plump and natty Oriental, sat alone at the distant end of the bar. The grinning teenager who had greeted them came from behind the bar with a tray, bottle of beer and glass, and glided through the gloom towards the driver.

'A hot time in the Miami Club tonight,' O'Malley said. 'What time's it warm up?'

'It has warmed up,' said the Colonel. 'There is a curfew.'

'Why'd they bother to stay open?'

The Colonel did not appear to be sure. 'The odd tourist? You can come and go so long as you are not on the streets. So long as you are not seen to be coming or going.'

'We saw plenty coming and going, didn't we?' And a few asleep, reflected O'Malley. On the pavements.

'Many exceptions. The curfew is not comprehensive. You need papers.' The Colonel gestured vaguely, raised his glass. 'Your health.'

'Yours. Good luck, Derry.'

A fragrance was spreading across the Superintendent's palate and up his nose. Was it the *tuba*, or the aroma from Colonel Rodrigo's waxed hair, or someone's herbal tobacco, or all of these whisked in with a peculiar perfumed smell of Asia which he believed he was beginning to identify as raisins? No, it was not, divined O'Malley. It was the Oriental who'd padded behind him with a drink and a yellow cigarette in one hand, and now was shaking the Colonel's hand with the other.

'Peter Tang,' the Colonel said, introducing. 'Superintendent O'Malley, Sergeant Maguire. Over from Ireland. Mr Tang is a pillar of our business community. Rotarian. Music-lover, I believe. Chairman of the Rizal Day Carnival Committee. Cement, is it not?'

'Cement,' confirmed Tang, and handed cards to O'Malley and Maguire. 'We handle two-fifths total manufacture in Philippines.'

For a moment O'Malley feared that the man was about to sell him cement. The fragrance Mr Tang exuded was not pomade because the round moon head was bald, but it might have been a head cologne for bringing out the highlights, or washing away grains of cement. The coil of smoke from the yellow joss-stick smelled of nutmeg and marjoram.

'Not glamorous commodity,' Tang was saying, 'not glamorous like police, yes. But we make living.'

'Bet you do,' O'Malley, much surprised, believed he heard Sergeant Maguire murmur.

'And yourselves,' Tang said, 'I begin to ask duty or pleasure, but can only be duty. Irish policemen rare in Manila. Most certainly unique I guess. Right, Colonel? You come take away that chap whatisname, Burke? Yes?'

The query was directed at O'Malley, who instead of saying 'Byrne' said nothing, and instead sipped from his glass. The spirit was adequately fiery and, like most other aspects of Manila he seemed to have come across in the past six hours, scented.

'One reads about your Mr Burke,' Tang said.

'He might have a bit of a reputation, I dare say.'

'He is at collusion with rebels, or so newspapers report. You cannot believe newspapers every time. I should know.' The upper lip curled like an ailing sandwich, and from beyond it splashed a watery sound which O'Malley identified as laughter. 'I have small interest in two newspapers.'

'That so?'

'Chinese-language. Most profitable sometimes. Not now because closed, all newspapers closed. Closed or censored. You enjoy your visit, sir?'

'Very much.'

'I pry,' said Mr Tang, and his mouth twisted into what may have been a deprecatory smile.

'Not at all.'

'Greatest blessings come disguised. Now Burke chap free, you free too I guess.'

O'Malley sipped.

'Excuse me, I try say, such brief acquaintance, but you do me honour, you both, lunch with me respectfully.' Mr Tang's mouth moulded into a sequence of contortions signifying, in turn, self-abasement, doubt, guilt, and finally winsomeness. 'So few Irish in Manila. We must give you good account.'

'You mean I get the bill?'

'Please?'

'Thanks,' O'Malley said, 'thanks a lot, but we're leaving tomorrow.'

'So soon? You cannot. Colonel, you persuade.'

'Here today, tomorrow,' said the Colonel, and completed the sentence with a gesture, floating his feminine palm through the air. 'You said it yourself, Mr Tang. We're more glamorous than cement.'

Mr Tang wagged the moon head. 'You change mind,

you have telephone number.' Detecting a blankness on the Superintendent's face, he added, 'On my card.'

'I will of course.'

'We would be civilized party,' Mr Tang said. 'You too, Colonel please, and dear friend of mine, Irish consul in Manila. Ireland is country of future I guess. Much building. One day we export cement. Very civilized party. I sure we satisfy each other.'

To avert the drowning sensation, the Superintendent looked long and hard at his watch. Mr Tang bowed, backed, and dissolved into the gloom.

'There's no Irish consulate here,' said O'Malley. 'Is there, Derry?'

While the Sergeant's mental processes tacked and circled prior to homing in on the question, the Colonel said, 'Could be an honorary consul. Unpaid and unknown. Turkey has one, and Ceylon. Like me to check?'

'No harm,' said O'Malley, and unhooked his ankles from the splats of the bar-stool. He put a Philippines banknote on the counter, and for good measure a second banknote on top of the first. He'd not got to grips yet with the currency and under the circumstances he wasn't going to bother, because if there was certainty or justice in the world, anyone accompanied by a Chief of Police was going to be returned shovelfuls of change. 'If we're having another round I'll try a beer. I'll just have a word with that pianist.'

Superintendent O'Malley walked through the half-dark, taking by surprise the lurking, flowery-shirted teenager who grinned and retreated into a patch of black. The piano was an upright. O'Malley hoisted an elbow on to its upper surface and stood, partly leaning, looking down at the pianist as though waiting for four bars intro-

duction, like Brendan O'Dowda, or Big John McCor-
mack.

'Don't stop,' O'Malley said, though the pianist not
only had not stopped but for the first time since the
policemen had entered the Miami Club had increased
the tempo. 'Last Saturday when you had the trouble.'
O'Malley had to speak loudly above the bounce of the
notes. Mood-music to feel suicidal to had become mood-
music to skip to. 'What did Burke sing? The Irishman,
remember?'

The pianist returned the policeman's gaze, saying nothing, but continuing to play. He was skinny and young,
and wore outside his slacks the obligatory open-necked,
short-sleeved shirt. Round one bony wrist was a copper
bracelet which in Dublin would have been for warding
off rheumatism, but here, O'Malley surmised, was adorn-
ment. The boy stared at him, playing. O'Malley supposed he was on drugs, and began to feel uncomfortable,
as though he were being made a fool of. The tune seemed
familiar.

'All I'm asking, sonny, is what he sang. Y'know who
I'm with over there?'

'Big shot cop,' the pianist said. 'I get two days of big
shot cops at Camp Crame. Big shot, little shot.'

'That's "Phil the Fluter's Ball",' O'Malley said.

But it was not, not any longer, for the tempo had
slowed to a weeping keening something or other which
was equally familiar but to which just for the moment
O'Malley couldn't put a name. Maguire and the Colonel
had joined him at the piano, the Sergeant passing over
beer and a fistful of change.

'What's this one called, Derry?'

' "Come Back to Erin".'

'That's it. Where'd you learn your repertoire, sonny? Was it the Irishman?'

'Is that what he was?' said the pianist. He took his hands from the keyboard, spread them on his knees, and stared down at them.

'Did he sing?'

'Some people like to sing.'

'How often did he come here?'

'When he felt like it. Mister, I had these questions. Two days, two nights in Camp –'

Colonel Rodrigo interrupted, speaking in a language O'Malley neither understood nor recognized. The pianist replied in presumably the same language. Sullen, eyes down, he said :

'Five, six times. I dunno. Not many times. He start to sing. I pick it up.'

'Good voice?'

'Sure.'

'How much'd he tip you?'

'Forty pesos. Fifty maybe.'

'Last Saturday –' O'Malley looked up sharply. 'Devil take it, what's going on?'

The clatter of a falling chair or table in the dark that shrouded the further end of the Miami Club, in the entrance area, was followed by shouts in the unknown language. There came a clipped squawking that might have been either human or animal, and the splintering of more furniture. 'Lights!' cried the Colonel, and he was darting towards the noise, hand digging in his holster, dapper feet kicking chairs out of his path.

The pianist side-stepped past O'Malley. Maguire

started after the Colonel.

'Derry!' O'Malley said, and Maguire halted. 'Wait awhile, lad. We'll keep outa this.'

A central light flooded the Miami Club. Apart from the Dublin policemen the sole tenants were the flowery-shirted teenager, one hand on a light-switch, and the boy barman in the white jacket, both hands round a shotgun. The barman was kneeling on the bar, his gun pointed beyond spilled furniture and broken glass towards the curtain. He saw O'Malley watching him but made no move to climb down or put away the gun.

Keep that thing pointed away from me, O'Malley wanted to tell him, but he told him nothing, apprehensive that anything he said might cause the gun to go off. To Maguire he murmured:

'I'd say it was bedtime. We're going to walk out and get a taxi, all right?'

' 'Tis none of our affair,' Maguire agreed.

Eyes on the barman, O'Malley had walked two paces when the curtain ahead parted and the Colonel came through, followed by the driver. The driver was dabbing at his temple with a crimson handkerchief. The barman clambered down behind the bar, the shotgun disappeared. Then the light went out.

'Put it on!' the Colonel barked, and light again engulfed the Miami Club.

The teenager assumed his grin, and abandoning the light-switch began to pick up chairs. Colonel Rodrigo walked energetically towards his guests.

'Drunks,' he explained.

Liar, thought O'Malley, though why he thought so he was not sure.

'I apologize,' the Colonel said. 'All your impressions

will be to our discredit.'

'We've a few lively ones of our own back home.'

'Perhaps we should follow suit.' The Colonel plucked a paper napkin from the bar and buffed his shoes. 'Would you care to move on? Guess we have lost our piano player.'

'I think we'll get back to the hotel. How's your driver?'

'He's all right. I'll drive.'

CHAPTER VII

O'MALLEY AWOKE from a sleep of variegated dreams. There'd been a hurley match in which he'd worn a flower-patterned shirt and been run off his feet, never getting so much as a tickle at the ball; a meaningless episode on a beach, throwing pebbles for a dog to retrieve; a suspiciously sexual and worrying encounter in a bathroom with a middle-aged and naked Filipino lady who'd told him to give a good account of himself; and a more relevant item, possibly, where he'd entered some manner of furniture shop and bumped into the Assistant Commissioner, who'd stabbed him in the chest with a finger, rhythmically, while singing in a throbbing bass, 'Come back to Erin, mavourneen, mavourneen,' over and over, interminably. O'Malley climbed out of bed, massaged his face, paying especial attention to the skin at the temples and above the eyes, and floundered through the dark in search of the curtain cord.

He found it. The double curtains swished apart. Sunlight dazzled him.

The room seemed a terrible height up in the air. A

mile or two directly below lay figures baking around a swimming-pool of brochure-blue. From under thatched umbrellas which sheltered, presumably, tables and tall drinks with straws, protruded occasional feet of pink, white or chocolate, and in one instance an elbow. Beyond the pool the town was a plateau of green lawns intersected by roads and sprinkled with sparkling concrete buildings : cement, O'Malley supposed, by courtesy of that Oriental fella, whatever his name was. A gaudy, chunky vehicle, he forgot its name, converted from an American wartime jeep and painted like a psychedelic fantasy, halted at a stop-light, and two girls stepped aboard. He remembered the name, jeepney, that was it, and felt reassured that his brain was beginning to function. He'd have enjoyed strolling for a day or two, being the tourist, while Rodrigo found Byrne. The centrepiece of one rectangle of greensward was fountains, in the middle of which, big as a hot-air balloon, stood a globe of the world. Beyond the lawns were more buildings, palms, parking lots, the waterfront, and the stifling sea.

Slid under the door of his room he found a morning newspaper and an envelope. In the envelope was a copy of a cable addressed to O'Mayla, Police HQ, Manila. It was from the Assistant Commissioner.

REMAIN MANILA STOP PHONE FULLEST
DETAILS SOONEST END

The *Manila Chronicle* across his lap (*Cruz Demands Probe Guilty Men*), O'Malley put in a call to Dublin Castle. He found Colonel Rodrigo's card in his wallet, recovered the newspaper, and dialled 59-99-28.

'My name's O'Malley. Could you give me Colonel Rodrigo?'

Getting the Colonel took a time. Senator Cruz, O'Malley saw, was not naming names, which spoke of caution, or perhaps the censorship mentioned by weed-smoking Tang. The guilty men remained anonymous. Anyhow, house arrest couldn't mean you were shut off from the Press, if Cruz was still under house-arrest. Eventually O'Malley got a Captain Tavera, or Taverna, who had a message, which turned out to be several messages, from the Colonel, who was out.

He would be back soon after mid-day, the Captain said, and had suggested lunch. Alternatively the invitation from Mr Tang was probably genuine if the Superintendent cared to pursue it. And an Irish consul was listed in the directory if he cared to pursue that : 40-38-21. Meanwhile the Colonel's office was at Mr O'Malley's disposal. Any facilities he might require, the original of the cable from Dublin, a car, secretary, he had only to ask Captain Taverna, or Tavera.

O'Malley thanked the Captain and hung up. The time was nine-ten. Take away eight. Starting with his little finger, O'Malley took away eight, and established that in Dublin the time was ten past one. In the morning. He was unconvinced. Where had those eight hours *gone*? At one-ten in the morning he'd probably get Dwyer, which wasn't an entrancing prospect. Dwyer or Corrigan. Or was he supposed to get on to Phoenix Park and speak fullest soonest with the AC himself? The cable hadn't been clear.

Discarding the newspaper, O'Malley snatched it up again, his eyes caught by two words, IRISHMAN FLEES. The incident had not been considered heart-stopping. Under the heading was a single mystifying paragraph at the foot of the page.

Patrick Burke, Irish singer and businessman domiciled in Manila, and now known to be sought by lawmen of many countries for international crimes, escaped yesterday from custody at Camp Crame. Despite sustained efforts by Constabulary investigators, Burke is believed to have been smuggled from the country by private plane. Superintendent O'Molly and Inspector Gwire of the Ireland Constabulary, in Manila to escort Burke back to Ireland, are expected to fly home today. O'Molly said: 'Burke has proved too clever for us.'

O'Malley blasphemed heartily. He read the paragraph again. Suffering Jesus, so much for discretion. Where the devil did they get it from? He read it a third time, smouldering, and began slowly to cool down. He shrugged and stood up. What did it matter? It wasn't as though the story was wholly inaccurate. Misleading, and gaps you could lose a foot in, but likely there was more truth in the piece than the newspaper guessed. Many of the villains O'Malley had known he had not disliked, but now for the first time he realized that he disliked Byrne, effortlessly.

He showered and shaved, working on himself briskly because of a powerful need for a mug of tea. He supposed he could have tea on the spot by phoning room service but he wasn't risking messing up the line with a call for tea when Dwyer might be wetting himself at the other end. Or with a call to Maguire, matter of that.

Maguire should sleep. The Superintendent observed a crack in the bathroom wall. Nothing serious, but a disappointment from a hotel of this class. The crack resembled a river system. Anna Liffey, with tributaries.

He had to telephone the switchboard to discover that there was a four-hour delay on his call to Dublin. 'Were you by any chance going to let me know,' O'Malley asked, 'or was I to be sitting here four hours with my embroidery, waiting?'

'Very good, sir,' drawled the operator with the ineffable non-communicativeness of one or two switchboard personnel whom O'Malley believed he'd come across before.

Peeved, desperate for tea, he abandoned and locked his room. Outside the door of the adjacent room, Maguire's, he set his ear against the wood and listened for sounds of revelry. There were none. He slid the cable under the door and took the lift to the Café Coquilla.

His bedside literature had applauded the Café Coquilla as a coffee-shop serving 'familiar favourites with a Spanish flair.' If they did coffee, reasoned O'Malley, they'd probably be able to muster a pot of tea, and though he'd not be dancing a jig about the Spanish flair, he was in a mood for familiar favourites, like rashers and eggs. He walked out of the lift into cool carpeted spaciousness inhabited by knots of guests, idle staff, and here and there an armed security guard. The directional signs for the lost were sawn-off segments of varnished planking into which the lettering – Rôtisserie, Reception, Port Orient, Coral Ballroom – had been burned with a hot implement. Entering the Café Coquilla, the first, second, third, fourth and fifth persons O'Malley observed, lingeringly, were waitresses : young, fragrant and disturbingly tender. The sixth person, alone, moody over remnants of breakfast, was Maguire.

'Hullo there, Inspector Gwire, and congratulations on the promotion. Didja see the papers?'

'I did, sir. Can you think why they didn't do our photos while they were about it?'

'Pressure of space, lad. Don't feel offended. Y'sleep at all?'

'I did, sir, thanks. A bit.'

'Grand, grand. We've a cable from Dublin, I put it under your door. I'm speaking to them at one, thereabouts, God and the switchboard willing. I'll not say I'm in raptures about the switchboard.'

He had hardly arranged himself in the chair across the table from Maguire when a waitress, efficient as well as a brown maid-goddess, was beside him with a menu. He waived the menu and requested tea, rashers, fried egg and toast, enunciating with resonant deliberation in case her language was not English but some goddess-tongue from a Philippine Olympus. He had to translate only the rashers. The enchantress left trippingly, trailing clouds of unattainable goddess-allure, backside jiggling under the trim mini-skirt.

'We could be outa here tonight, lad. We'll see the Colonel fella later. I'd not mind asking a question or two at that Clark Airbase, but 'tis likely miles away. Have y'had breakfast?'

'Sausages and stuff.'

'So where's our wandering Paddy? Where's our boy, then? D'ye think he'll be still in the Philippines?'

'If he is, I've a feeling we'll not be seeing him, not this side of Christmas. My opinion's a wasted journey, sir, if

you're askin'. The spite'll be flyin' when they get to
counting the pennies back home. There's a package for
you.' Maguire took from his briefcase a packet the size
of a half-pound chocolate-box, wrapped in brown paper
and tied with string. 'They gave me it at the desk like
they were happy to be shut of it.'

'What d'ye mean?' O'Malley turned the package over
in his hands. There was no stamp. The designation was
printed in black ballpoint and correctly spelled: *Superintendent O'Malley, Manila Hilton. By Hand.* He shook
the packet a trifle gingerly, holding it to his ear. 'We're
expecting no bombs are we, Derry?'

'Nor birthday presents either as I know of.'

O'Malley gave his assistant a thoughtful look. 'Unless
you're being alarmist, perhaps you'd best dunk it in a
bucket of water.' He put the packet in front of the Sergeant.

' 'Tis no bomb, sir, I'd swear to that. I did the explo-
sives course last April.'

'Did you now.' O'Malley leaned back, allowing the
virgin goddess to arrange cutlery and tea in front of him.
When she had tripped away he leaned forward. 'You
open it then, and I'll be watching like this, at close range,
so if you're wrong we'll go up together.'

Maguire untied the string and with orderly movements unfolded the brown paper. A chocolate-box stood
revealed: Bato's Pecan Parfait, the pictorial design a
festoon of leaves, possibly pecan leaves. Draping a handkerchief over the box like a conjuror, the Sergeant eased
the lid upwards and off. Inside was packing of red wet
tissues, which came away more or less in a sodden lump.
Under them, in the bottom of the box, was a human
hand. A copper bracelet circled it, bisecting the knuckles

of the second and third fingers and pressing into the flesh
of the bloody stump where once the wrist had been.

'Cover it up, lad,' O'Malley said.

He watched the Sergeant replace tissues, lid and
brown paper, then looked round for the waitress, hoping
to catch her before she brought the rashers and eggs.

CHAPTER VIII

THE PACKAGE sat on the shelf above the refrigerator in
O'Malley's room. O'Malley sat on the unmade bed, telephoning. Maguire knocked on the unlocked door and
walked in.

He carried the Byrne file. Averting his eyes from the
package, he dropped the file on the bed beside O'Malley
and wandered to the window. The view over lawns, car
parks and the harbour was the same as from his own
room. The room itself was the same, identically decorated and furnished even to the undisturbed half-pint of
rum, and likely, considered Maguire, with the same
earthquake cracks in the bathroom. Thoughts jostling
for admittance to the Sergeant's travel-worn mind,
thoughts he felt sure would be pertinent once they de-
clared themselves, were held back by one insistent, futile
query. Was *By Hand,* Sergeant Maguire wanted to know,
an instruction or a joke?

O'Malley was asking Captain Taverna to tell the
Colonel, as soon as he could be located, that the left hand
of the Miami Club pianist had come into his possession.

On another planet, far below, a bronzed convention
of bankers were coyly wrestling at the edge of the swim-

ming-pool, competing in pushing one another into the water.

'Thoughts, lad?'

'We don't know it's the pianist. But I'd bet on it.'

'You'll not find a taker. We don't know Byrne's the butcher either, but I'd bet on that. Evens. Anything else?'

'I'm beginning to miss Dublin.'

The Dublin detectives stood by the window, staring out at the Asian heat. On the planet below, with an unheard shout and splash, a banker hit the transparent blue. Maguire's thoughts began to marshal themselves.

'I couldn't find the cable.'

'I slid it under your door.'

'It's not there.'

'Damn.' O'Malley groped for his handkerchief, but too late to contain the sneeze. 'Is the room made up yet?'

'Not yet. There are some maids up the corridor. Could you have got the wrong door?'

'I'm three seventy-four, you're three seventy-five. Aren't you?'

'I am. Nothing else has been touched, far as I can see. Do we tell the manager?'

'Suppose so. Much good it'll do.' O'Malley blew his nose. Three psychedelic jeepneys, passengers spilling from back and sides, were careering in convoy past the lawns where stood the globe of the world. 'So why bother. For the same reason we don't switch hotels. Someone's got his eye on us, lad. We're being harassed.'

'I'd a phone-call last night, but they hung up.'

'I had three,' O'Malley said, and sneezed again, volcanically. 'God save us.'

'Was that commotion in the Miami Club,' Maguire

said, 'a bit of the harassment too, would y'say?'

'From the feel of it, Derry, I'd say this city sets records for commotions. What was going on in the Miami place I couldn't tell you. What did y'make of the Chinese fella? The one asked us to lunch?'

'I'd not trust him with a bus-fare. Matter of fact, sir, I was going to ask you the same. You saw what he was drinking?'

'He wasn't. He had a glass and he never touched it, like he thought it was poisoned. Not a sip.'

'That so?' Maguire had not noticed. 'Well I sipped it, after he'd gone, because it looked funny stuff to me. It was water.'

'A Chinese water-drinker. Who won't touch water. So what's he doing at the bar of the Miami Club?'

'Asking us to lunch?'

'So we'll accept. You've got his card, phone him, see if tomorrow's all right. With any luck we'll be saving the taxpayer a pair of lunch vouchers. Now, here's what else we do.' O'Malley walked to the bed and picked up the Byrne file. 'First we pay our respects to the manager of this pub, if he's around. We're ambassadors for Ireland, Derry, and you never know, he might have had a cable handed in. Then we split. I've a coupla jobs for you. I'm taking a stroll to see this honorary Irish consul, whoever he is. Apart from being a mate of Tang, if we believe Tang. Do you believe Tang?'

'Not particularly.'

'No. Well. I'll not be losing sleep over Tang. If the consul's Irish he should have something to say about Byrne, even if 'tis only he's a poor misunderstood hounded patriot. We'll meet back here at twelve and make our phone calls.'

He handed the Byrne file to Maguire.

'Look after that. Lock it up. There's nothing in it of any use, and whoever nicked the cable knows it, or he'd have demolished your room while he was about it and gone off with the file and your case and everything. But we're not going back home having to say our pockets were picked.'

'You think pinching the cable's just trying to warn us off, like the phone calls and, ah – ' unwillingly the Sergeant's eyes moved to the package over the refrigerator – 'the piano-player.'

'Right now, lad, I don't know anything about anything, except I've had no breakfast, and for all we know this room's bugged.'

The harassment works, Maguire thought. First morning in Spook-city of the Orient and it's talk of the room being bugged.

'So call Tang,' the Chief was saying. 'Then get a schedule of all flights out in the direction of Dublin, just in case. Change our rooms if you want. If we're seeing the manager I might as well mention it. And bring that thing.'

'Bring what thing?' Maguire said, though he knew.

Rather than voice the four-letter word, the Superintendent started to gesture towards the package, but the gesture became a swooping movement for his handkerchief. His nostrils tickled, spasms accumulated. Maguire waited. The sneeze tromboned into the handkerchief. O'Malley swore, dabbed eyes and nose.

'That thing,' he said. 'You can get a carrier-bag at that newspaper-stand. Put it on expenses.'

Bruce Diamond, manager of the Manila Hilton, was a

bony, optimistic Australian who felt it his duty not only to promote the hotel but to praise and defend against all-comers the fabled city in which it stood. He performed the latter task with an aggressive protesting energy that left O'Malley wanting to advise on the dangers of overkill.

'Intramuros, that's a must, the old walled city, Spanish, it'll knock you out,' Diamond said, and he strode through a door bearing the title Barrio Hilton.

Behind, grimacing to restrain further sneezes, walked O'Malley; then Sergeant Maguire, holding by the string handles a plastic carrier-bag with the inscription *Capiz Boutique*.

'Next, the Luneta, go about half-five.' Diamond motioned his guests into bamboo chairs, seated himself in a third, and handed a visiting-card to each Irishman. They were at the pool's side, above their heads an umbrella of thatch. O'Malley wondered if he would be expected to swim. 'Half-five, six,' Diamond said, 'you tell me if ever you've seen a sunset like it, anywhere.'

'The sunset's grand, we saw it last night,' O'Malley said.

'A real beaut,' Maguire murmured, scratching at mosquito bites on his calf.

'Too bad you gentlemen have picked right now, I'm away to Tokyo after lunch.' The manager wore bifocals and a spruce navy blazer. Needlessly, for at least two girls were threading towards him with pencils and menu-cards, he glanced round, hand aloft for service. 'Policy conference, dammit. Back Sunday. All I want ever is to stay right here. There's no place like the Philippines and I've seen the best of three continents. Smell that air.'

O'Malley smelled nothing through his stuffed nose.

Maguire lifted his head, sniffed, and identified one part chlorine, two parts suntan oil.

'Whether you find this guy or not, you take yourselves out into the country,' Diamond said. 'That's if you want to meet the real Filipinos. Tough as teak and charm like you wouldn't know existed. Living off a bowl of rice a day, most of 'em. It's the metabolism. Down in Mindanao they're stone-age. Actual stone-age. You'll need a guide. Look, I'm going to have you meet Bob Scott, he's my right hand here. Coffee, tea? Something stronger?'

Maguire, who at the mention of right hand had involuntarily lowered his eyes towards the carrier-bag, now looked at the pool. Two bankers' wives in bathing-caps had taken over from the bankers and were swimming a lugubrious breaststroke across the pool, and back again, in unison, stroke for stroke. Then across once more, heaving themselves onward, trailing bubbles and tossed water-beads, a doleful chlorine-spouting marathon, unregarded by the bleached husbands nursing bourbon and dozing under paisley eye-shades.

Steering the subject away from the sights of the Philippines, the Super was asking Diamond if he'd come across a citizen named Tang, but he hadn't. He hadn't heard of the Miami Club either, but he spoke well of *tuba*, and the pranks of the fun-loving Filipinos when under its influence. No, he hadn't been aware there was an Irish consul. No, Burke, or Byrne or whoever struck a chord, but faintly, and if the bloke had been a regular of any of the Hilton's bars, he'd have known. Ewart Hart? Everyone knew about him. A tin-god demagogue who lived in the hills with the savages and fed them lies and guns. He'd stop a bullet one day, sooner the better.

Tea arrived, and slices of lime. The manager looked at

his watch. Only when O'Malley mentioned that a cable was missing from the Sergeant's room did the Australian throw off the torpor which had settled on him since the conversation had veered away from the tourist circuit.

'You sure?'

'Afraid so.'

'Can't believe it. Our staff's as one hundred per cent loyal as you'll find anywhere. They know when they're well off and they play along. The guests, well, you can't get a security clearance on every client who walks in, but we get the pick here. Our complaint ratio is negligible. You want to know? I'd be surprised if you didn't find that cable.'

'Well, I don't think – '

'When you do you'll be kicking yourself.'

' 'Tis possible there's – '

'You don't know the hotel business, O'Malley. The people we get mislaying things. I could tell you some cases.'

' 'Tis not important at all.'

'I can't agree with you there,' Diamond said fiercely. 'An accusation is an accusation, and if there's a rotten apple here, I'm not saying there is, but we have a reputation second to none. I'll have Bob Scott take on this one. Bob'll get to the bottom of it. Nothing that can be done's going to be left unturned, I can promise you that.'

O'Malley exhaled windily through his mouth : the sigh of the liberated. He stood with the Sergeant at the head of an escalator and watched the manager march away into administrative darkness.

'You didn't mention about changing our rooms, sir,' Maguire said.

'Lost my nerve,' said O'Malley.

A six-foot Caucasian blonde with a chest like the north face of the Eiger stepped past the policemen and on to the escalator. O'Malley put the manager's card into his wallet.

'In his job he must meet thousands,' he said. 'Can he really not have met a social swinger like Paddy Byrne?'

'We don't know for certain Byrne's a social swinger, sir. Do we?' Maguire swapped the carrier-bag from one hand to the other. 'We know he's no halfwit. If he's been lifting guns from the Yanks and selling half of 'em to these Maoists, and the other half to the IRA – '

'Or the Provos.'

'Or the North. Or anyone with a cheque-book. Well, if he was into all that he'd lie pretty low, wouldn't he?'

'Social singer, then. You'll not deny he's fond of the spotlight, given the chance.'

'I'll not. But we don't know how he goes courtin' it.' The Sergeant smoothed his moustache with the knuckles of his unoccupied hand. ' 'Tis possible it's the singing not the spotlight he's mad for. Like some must smoke, or tell jokes.'

'Or flog Intramuros by sunset,' said O'Malley, gazing in the wake of the vanished manager. 'Does it not sound like one of those Continental football teams? Intramuros, two : Bayern Munich, seven.'

The pair rode the escalator down to the lobby. Clients sauntered with shopping-bags, golf-bags, pigskin brief-cases, packed lunches for coach tours into the safer regions of the interior. A bellhop trundled a trolley stacked with baggage. In the gloom of a blind alcove lounged two guards, guns slung over shoulders.

'So we believe the manager,' O'Malley said.

They walked slowly through the lobby in the direction of the hotel entrance.

'I didn't hear him say anything interesting enough to disbelieve,' said Maguire. 'Very competent manager, I wouldn't wonder. Unless it's vital, sir, I'd be happy not to have to meet Bob Scott.'

'Derry, I give my oath, I'll protect you from Bob Scott. So. But we don't seem to be making much progress.'

They halted on the broad step outside the entrance. Glinting products from General Motors and Ford's glided into the forecourt, and drew away. One more pace forward and the Dublin detectives would have crossed the Rubicon which divided *sol* from *ombre*. O'Malley said:

'He could be smuggled out of the country. Or cowerin' in some cellar fifty yards from here. Or shacked up in style with whoever the Croesus is who bought him his ticket out of Camp Crame. If Colonel Rodrigo knows what he's talking about. When you come to think of it, we don't know much.'

'Devil we do, sir.'

'But we know he's no halfwit, and we know he's cracked, and I don't care for that. 'Tis an ugly combination. If I was Dublin, lad, I'll tell you, I'd leave him be. Let these fellas here look out for him. He's a boyo the ould country can do without.'

'I'd take him back and have him locked in the Bog so's he can sing to the four walls and a high window. Till the year two thousand.'

O'Malley looked sideways at the Sergeant. His assistant was grave-faced, fondling the dreadful moustache.

'Since we haven't got him to take back,' O'Malley said,

'you can take that article to Colonel Rodrigo's office instead. My compliments. I'm away for a jar with the consul.'

Sergeant Maguire frowned down at the carrier-bag, lifted it an inch, lowered it.

'The Red Hand of Ulster,' he said.

'Don't be smart, lad. Get on with it. And don't get lost.'

'With respect, sir, I wasn't being smart. Historically the Red Hand – '

'Sergeant! 'Tis too warm altogether. Look lively now. Back here about twelve sharp.'

Persecuted Maguire sulked into the sun and along the street. He knew a thing or two about heraldry. If the Super didn't want to learn, so much for that, the thick ox. Badge of the Black North the Red Hand was, swiped from the coat of arms of the lords O'Neill, oldest family in Europe, rulers of Ulster for twelve centuries, descendants of the kings of Tara. What was wrong with that for an observation?

When Maguire halted to rub his chewed and itching calf against the back of his leg, the car creeping after him on the far side of the road, tyres scraping the kerb, halted also. When he walked on, the car crept on.

The arms of the North had the Red Hand slap in the centre, in a star, with a crown on top. Red lion and Irish elk, and banners with harp and cross, to left and right. Or right and left. And the South's coat of arms had the Red Hand bottom left. A cross gules, in escutcheon argent charged with a dexter hand couped at the wrist also gules. Something like that, that was how the heraldry fellers'd talk about it. The wrapped hand weighing down the *Capiz Boutique* bag was sinister, not dexter, but it was couped at the wrist right enough.

Morose, reluctant to accept that his observation was interesting but worthless, Sergeant Maguire turned into police headquarters. The car parked at the kerbside, illegally, but unmolested.

CAPTER IX

RED HAND of Ulster my granny, grumbled O'Malley, striding along United Nations Avenue with the Irish consul's address in one hand, Manila street map in the other. He might have snorted his derision had his nose not been blocked with the sudden, villainous cold. Fit as a tinker's dog all year, he complained to street map. Moment you reach the tropics, a pouring cold. The climate was an incubator for germs.

'Shoeshine, mister?'

O'Malley walked on, deaf to the urchin. Trouble with this young crop of sergeants was they found symbols under the bed. Symbols, psychology, sociology. Give a sprat like Maguire the chance and he'd be arguing for rehabilitation centres with telly and classrooms. For scum like Byrne.

No, that wasn't quite fair. Locking Byrne in the Bog till the year Two thousand, that showed the right spirit. Not that you'd any alternative if you weren't going to top him, and nuts like him, and no one with a crumb of Holy Catholic sense could think of doing that. There was good stuff in Maguire.

But what did the Red Hand of Ulster have to do with

anything? Byrne, or one of his hatchet-men, subtle as tar and feathers, had presented the pianist's hand by way of advice to stop sniffing about and get out. That was it and that was all.

Unless Maguire had a point. And Byrne was announcing he was still in the game, on the side of Ulster, and any nosey-parker Republican Irish, like O'Malley and Maguire, rozzers to boot, were on his list.

In which case, O'Malley gloomily concluded, I ought to have thought of it first, not let that spark come out with it, him with his travel-fatigue and moustache.

'Hey, Joe, shine your shoes?'

'Joe, shoeshine?'

The unbroken voices were American, the features and nut-coloured skin were Filipino. They sat bare-chested in a puddle of shade, a grinning, beckoning, lethargic huddle of boys without, as far as O'Malley could see, brushes or polish. Further on he responded curtly to a child touting lottery tickets. He side-stepped two characters in dark glasses approaching from the opposite direction, hand clamping mechanically over his breast pocket as they brushed past. Sunglasses, straw hats, wide-nosed Malay faces, Chinese faces, women with bare arms, men in slacks and canvas shoes, smells of frying and petrol, an elderly white man with a briefcase, blue-uniformed security guards in doorways, American cars, Japanese cars, a convoy of four troop-filled army trucks, in the gutter a beggar with upturned palms, the plate glass of the Catholic Travel Center, American Express Company, First National City Bank of America, Arpex Travel Service, KLM Royal Dutch Airlines, S. C. Vizcarra Arts & Handicrafts, American Chamber of Commerce. The heat pressed against O'Malley like a furry skin. At Taft

Avenue, an intersecting canyon of glass and white cement (by Tang Cement Inc., wondered O'Malley), he
paused, looked up for street numbers, down at the
creased map. An urchin plucked his sleeve.

'Marihuana?'

'Go home.'

'Girl? Nice virgin?'

'Gwan, gerronout.'

'Blue movie?'

'I said out. Why aren't you at school?'

'Marihuana, mister. Only twenty pesos.'

To read the brass plaques in the entrance to the Soncom Development Corporation Building, O'Malley had
to ask the security guard to shift aside a bit. The man
looked old to be a guard, in Dublin he might have been
a nightwatchman with sandwiches in a paper bag, and to
O'Malley's inexpert eye his gun looked antique, a fowl-
ing-piece from an earlier age, a collector's item requiring
accessories such as ramrod, powder-horn, and crucible
for moulding bullets. Could the long barrel be made of
iron? The almost equally long stock was of wood: dull
and smooth as though handled by generations of Filipinos from the time of the Spanish-American War, or
Magellan.

M. Reyes

Investment Consultant

Consulate of the Republic of Ireland

7th Floor

O'Malley bestowed on the guard a manic smile and
advanced into the building. His back felt as exposed as a

shooting-gallery. Behind him the guard, rheumy and inscrutable, uttered a throat-clearing sound. O'Malley was conscious that the firearm was not necessarily the less lethal for being a relic. He ducked nimbly into the lift and rode to the seventh floor with a child operator who either was unarmed or kept his guns concealed.

He debouched on to a landing with directional numbers and arrows, knocked on a door's frosted glass, and walked into an office the size of a ship's lounge. Judging from the two doors leading off, the lounge was only the beginning. At a desk under the window a scowling man was scissoring a pink newspaper which the Superintendent assumed to be the *Financial Times*. At another desk a girl was typing and munching, her bitten apple in repose like a still-life beside the typewriter. Riffling through papers in a filing-cabinet stood a handsome fortyish woman with black hair pulled back from her forehead and clasped by an amber gewgaw at the nape of her neck. All three were Filipino, all three looked up.

'Morning. Name's O'Malley. I was wondering, would I be right now, I'm looking for the Irish consul.'

Should have said that in the Gaelic, that'd have been an entrance, he thought, ignoring the fact that his knowledge of the Irish language had grown so threadbare over the years that it now comprised the merest rags of phrases. No Irish flags, he noticed, no wall-maps, calendars with Martello towers, portraits of the President taking his ease in Aras an Uachtarain. Couple of abstract paintings, meagre on paint but reaching across half a wall. An excess of cushioned furniture, carpet, veneer. Smell of manufactured sweetness, as though entering a toffee factory.

'I am honorary consul,' said the woman at the filing cabinet. 'Is it a passport matter?'

'Oh,' O'Malley said. 'Hullo. No.'

'I have not the authority for passports. We have a local agreement with the British Embassy.'

'Not the American?'

'No,' the woman said with a startled look, as though the question had never been raised before. 'The British, you should try there, they're very helpful. One-four, one-four, Roxas Boulevard.'

'Matter of fact it's not the passport.' O'Malley opened and held out for the consul his warrant card. 'I'll not be keeping you five minutes.'

She led the way into an inner office, the amber clasp in her hair glinting as she walked through sunshine that poured in at the window. Her dress, wide vertical stripes of chocolate and orange, might have given an illusion of an extra inch of height, but she was clearly little more than five feet tall. Even more clearly, to O'Malley, she was a good-looker who'd looked after herself. Closing the door, she motioned her caller to a leather chair with footstool, and after some moments of delving and sifting in drawers, handed him two visiting-cards. One designated M. Reyes as Investment Consultant, Soncom Development Corporation Building, Taft Avenue, Tel. 40-38-21. The other, which she had to hunt for, established her as Honorary Irish Consul of the same address.

'You have just arrived in Manila, Mr ah – '

'O'Malley,' O'Malley said, wondering whether Ireland might be rare or peculiar (or advanced, why in hell shouldn't the old country be advanced in this one particular?) in being without the visiting-card. At least in the circles he moved in. 'Last night.'

'If you wish to ask about this person Burke, I'm afraid I can be of little help.'

'Ah. You know about him.'

'I read the papers.'

'Have you met him ever?'

'Never.'

That, thought O'Malley, sounds final enough. 'He's never called on you for any sort of assistance?'

'Why would he?'

'As an Irish national.'

'No. I saw him once. Singing.'

'When was that?'

'I suppose about six months ago. Was it Easter? A concert at the John Hay Airbase.'

'What did he sing? D'ye remember?'

'Heaven no.' Her expression became amused and patronizing, as though she had entered into conversation with a stray child. 'Odd question.'

'You never can tell. Was it the opera, f'rinstance?'

'Irish songs, I'm sure. Tiddly-aye-tye-tye. You know?'

'I know.' O'Malley nodded knowledgeably. He wondered if he would be offered tea. 'Was he popular?'

'So far as I remember. Not so popular as the stripper, but who could have been?' She smiled, and her fingertips played along the neck of her dress. 'The audience was fairly uncritical.'

'Americans?'

'Mostly. As you know, Camp Hay is the recreation centre for their troops.'

'Might I ask you,' asked O'Malley, who hadn't known, 'why you were there?'

'I was invited. I have been several times. Some of our clients, our investment clients, are servicemen.'

'Who runs the recreation bit? That's to say, these concerts, who puts the acts together? D'ye know?'

'No.'

'What about the top man there, have y'met him?'

'Major Saunders. We have met at functions. The compère was a Lieutenant Ball. He made too many jokes about his name. I did not find them funny.'

'Did you not?' O'Malley, fidgeting with the visiting-cards, stared at the carpet. Not only did his bunged nostrils tickle but his eyes had started to water. 'So that's the only time you've seen Burke.'

'Yes.'

'What about television, has he sung there?'

'Not that I know of. But I never watch, our programmes are very fourth-rate. Basketball and dubbed westerns, y'know? I'm sorry, Mr O'Malley. You have come from Ireland to collect this man?'

'That was the plan.'

'He must be important. I suppose there's no reason why I should have been informed.'

'None really,' O'Malley agreed. He wondered in what forgotten file in Stephen's Green resided the name M. Reyes, and who if anyone would have thought to look, and whether the lady was piqued or relieved not to have been informed. 'On Saturday the constabulary took him in. What I was getting at, it was possible he might have tried to speak to you. Or you'd visited him.'

'Mr O'Malley, the first I knew this individual was in Camp Crame was this morning when I read he had escaped. If he has joined the rebels you will have to collect him from the hills.'

'Did the papers say he'd joined the rebels? My

Chronicle thought he'd been smuggled out of the country.'

The smile surfaced again, the consul's hands clasped each other upon the desk : slender cinnamon-coloured fingers for tabulating share prices and telephoning investors. A sapphire ring encircled the fourth finger of the right hand, leaving O'Malley pondering whether this might be the Philippines finger for wedding-rings. He looked beyond her to a wall where hung a portrait of the President : not the Irish President but the Philippines President, smoothly-barbered, unsmiling, icily benevolent, a very present help in time of trouble. There were bookcases, a vase erupting with bougainvillaea.

'If you had been in the Philippines a little longer you would have learned to recognize our newspaper shorthand. Anyone joining the rebels is reported as having left the country. Or more usually is not reported at all. The government is unenthusiastic about recruits to the opposition.'

'Are they unenthusiastic about me?'

'Why would they be?'

'The paper I saw said my assistant and I were heading back for Ireland. Today.' O'Malley thirsted for tea. His eyes roved in quest of a gas-ring, kettle, packet of Brooke Bond. 'How many papers d'you have in Manila?'

'At present I think only the *Chronicle*.' She spread an apologetic hand. 'Normally six or seven maybe. But these are not normal times. Unreliable papers are closed down, temporarily.'

'So why does the *Chronicle* think we're off home?'

'You must ask them. If your trip no longer has a point, it seems a reasonable guess. Are you not going back today?'

' 'Tis possible. Then again we might stay on awhile. Look around. We're invited to lunch with a friend of yours. Peter Tang.'

'Oh? You know him?'

'A passing encounter.'

'You will lunch well. Mr O'Malley, I am sorry not to be able to help you with this Burke. Perhaps if you and Sergeant Maguire were to try the constabulary, or better still our Manila police. Even in these pitiful times we have still some honest men in the city police. Or you might do worse than ask Mr Tang. He has contacts, I understand.'

The hands unclasped and she stood up, princess-sized. There came a knock at the door and the scowling man appeared, in his hand a square of paper torn from the teleprinter.

'I'll be with you,' the consul told him.

The man withdrew. The consul escorted O'Malley, unwilling, towards the door. The chocolate and orange shimmered through the rod of sunlight. French perfume mingled with the toffee odours.

'Tin up a point?' O'Malley said.

'I beg your pardon?'

'Price of tin. How's the investment world?'

'Erratic,' the consul said shortly. 'We have some recovery but there are rumours the rebels are regrouping. We would like to be sure they are only rumours.'

'Wouldn't you have to have a word with Mr Hart about that?'

'The tiresome Mr Hart. Many people would like a word with Mr Hart.'

They arrived in the outer office at the moment the munching girl tossed her apple core into a waste-basket.

The man stood in a crouch over the stuttering teleprinter.

'So what, like I was wondering,' O'Malley said, 'd'ye
find to do as Irish consul?' Accustomed to choosing
when interviews should end, he had been left frustrated
and irritated by the consul's closing of this one. His
mouth was dry as the pavements along Taft Avenue.
'Mean to say, you can't have that many Irish here.'

'Mostly nuns. Very occasionally tourists. I am only
honorary consul, you understand. There is little to do,
and no salary.'

'But cash for our stranded hippies, that sorta thing.'

'Twice I have authorized loans.'

'Right of asylum.'

'Asylum? Are we talking of Burke again?'

'No, no. No one in particular. Just curiosity. Might I
ask why you are consul? D'you know Ireland at all?'

'Poorly. I studied for a post-graduate year at your
UCD.'

'That so?' He waited for her to elaborate.

'Moral Sciences,' she elaborated, and held out her
hand.

'I'm on my way, so.' O'Malley gripped and released
the cool hand. 'Thank you, madam. Obliged.'

'Goodbye, Mr O'Malley.'

He descended in the elevator and walked past the
guard into the glare of Taft Avenue. He was angry and
thirsty. Why was the woman such a liar? Why should
the Irish honorary consul of all people lie to a visiting
Irish policeman? Moral Sciences. Did University Col-
lege have such a course? Perhaps they did. Maguire
might know.

But 'Sergeant Maguire'. He'd not mentioned Sergeant Maguire. Where'd the woman heard of Sergeant Maguire if her only source of information had been the *Chronicle*, which knew no Sergeant Maguire, only an Inspector Gwire?

CHAPTER X

'DERRY, you in there?'

Detective-Superintendent O'Malley, jacket draped damply over forearm, knocked on the door of his bathroom. Grey, hot, glistening, he put his ear to the door. When no one answered he looked in, and sneezed into emptiness.

He returned to the corridor and knocked on Maguire's door. Nothing. From his own room he phoned Maguire's room. He found an amiable chambermaid who unlocked Maguire's room, establishing that it was empty. Pyjamas were there. Locked suitcase. The Sergeant had not had the rooms changed.

The time was only a little past mid-day. O'Malley closed the door of his room, hung the inappropriate jacket on the back of a chair, and poured a long drink of water from the vacuum-jug. The Sergeant could be sunning himself, or out shopping for mementos. Fertility masks, carved water-buffalo, knick-knacks for the relations. O'Malley was unconvinced.

'Damn,' he said, and dialled police headquarters. Twice he was transferred before being put on to a duty officer in the detective division.

Yes, Captain Taverna was out. No, Colonel Rodrigo

was not yet back. Yes, the Irish Sergeant Maguire had brought a packet, it was in the Colonel's office. No, the Sergeant Maguire had not said where he was going. No, he'd not left any message.

O'Malley dialled reception. No messages.

'Damn.'

He ferreted among visiting cards, and dialled Tang's number. A female voice answered, measured and competent. Mr Tang was out but yes, Mr Maguire had spoken with him, lunch tomorrow, rendezvous at noon at the Hilton, the Harana cocktail lounge. Then to Mr Tang's residence in Bel Air.

O'Malley phoned room service for a pot of tea. He took a shower and put on a fresh shirt, his third and last, then sat by the window, drinking tea, brooding, looking at the bathers below, the globe of the world, the dusty mirror that was the sea. When the phone shrilled he was out of the chair like a cat after a rat.

'Hullo there, yes?'

It was some department of management, bills presumably, a girl's voice inquiring whether he and Mr Maguire would be checking out today.

'I couldn't tell you that. I'll let you know. Later. Listen, 'twould be a service if you could get on to the switchboard for me. What I'm after wondering is, d'you think you could discover about a call I have in to Dublin, Ireland. Name's O'Malley. Room three-seven-four. If you could manage a supervisor. Happen she'll take notice of you. I've been waitin' since the days of the primeval ooze.'

Five minutes later the phone rang. It was the switchboard, and another female voice, American-accented.

'Your call to Dublin, sir?'

'Grand. Right away. Thanks.'

'Sorry, sir, there is a delay on all calls to Dublin.'

'Arrah, what's it now? There've been delays since I got here. How much longer?'

'A moment, please.' After many moments the voice said, 'Probably tomorrow at the latest.'

'Tomorrow! Are y'telling me I've to wait till tomorrow? Listen now, would you listen. My name's O'Malley, Superintendent – '

'A moment, please.'

The moment plodded into minutes. O'Malley chafed, breathed hard, flexed his fingers, clenched his jaw muscles.

'Hullo,' said the voice.

'Yes?'

'There's a fault on the cable, sir, they're trying to trace it.'

'What,' said O'Malley, holding his voice steady, 'class of a fault?'

'A moment, please.'

'Wait! Hullo?'

O'Malley's eyes rolled upwards, his tongue and lips blasphemed. He sat down heavily on the bed, the phone in his hand. He stood up again. Eventually she returned, her voice calm, matter-of-fact. It was a voice that would remain impregnably matter-of-fact even at the Last Trump when the four horsemen were galloping through the firmament and the world was crumbling in ashes.

'They won't know until they have traced it, sir.'

O'Malley dabbed his face with his handkerchief. His hand was clammy round the receiver. 'Would you get me the Manila police? Hold on, I've a number.'

He collected his wallet from his jacket and retrieved

the phone. 'What you're telling me is,' he said, sifting one-handed through cards, 'I've no way of communicating with Dublin until this cable's mended, which could be tomorrow, amn't I right? What about satellites, though? Can't you route the call by satellite, or through Tokyo or Hong Kong or somewhere? You're not after telling me because one of your cable's banjaxed there's no phoning Dublin? What if there was war, wouldn't you find a way? If it's an extra quid by satellite, don't worry about that, I have the pesos. Hullo? Hullo?'

O'Malley stabbed savagely at the buttons.

'Hullo! Madam!'

Silence.

He crashed down the handset, thrashed it up and down, and lifted it.

'You have the number, sir?'

'What number?'

'You had a number for the police?'

'Listen, this call to Dublin. Don't vanish off now. It's what you might describe as important. Priority, you might say. Now, can you not beam it off a satellite?'

'Not until the storm is passed, sir.'

'Ah.' O'Malley looked through the window at the day's bright calm. 'A storm is it?'

'There has been electrical interference for two days, sir.'

Without warning the voice grew technical, embarking on an unsolicited lecture about circuits and high frequency radio signals. O'Malley caught the word 'ionosphere'. He declined an offer to be put through to weather forecasts, but asked, when the voice paused for breath, whether he might send a telegram, since he couldn't telephone. The lecture took up the question with a diversion into the subject of printed symbol transmission as opposed to voice transmission. Both, O'Malley gathered, under present conditions, were equally impossible.

'Because you've electrics in the ionosphere,' said O'Malley, 'and clinkers in your cable.'

'The cable fault is at Dublin, sir.'

'Would you get me this Manila number? Five-nine double-nine two-eight.'

It was accomplished. Colonel Rodrigo apologized for having only that moment got back. He thanked the Superintendent for the package, and suggested he call at headquarters as soon as possible. There had been one or two developments.

'The development here is my sergeant's missing,' O'Malley said. 'We were to meet at twelve. It's one now.'

He waited to be told that Maguire was with the Colonel, or down the road buying colour slides of sunset over Corregidor.

'I'll put out an all-cars call,' the Colonel said. 'Is there any hope you have his photograph?'

The Colonel's efficiency impressed O'Malley. By the time the Irishman walked into the Police Chief's office, barely fifteen minutes after putting down the phone, three reports had come in of persons approximating to the description of a moustached, blue-eyed pale-complexioned European : height five eleven, eyes blue, age twenty-nine, wearing a brown double-breasted suit and tie. Roughly such a person was being escorted into the office at the moment O'Malley entered, though he was

over six feet tall and dressed in slacks and a linen jacket.
A Mercedes representative named Gunther Weiss, the
person insisted, and flourished documents in evidence.
O'Malley anticipated unpleasantness, but the Colonel
charmed Herr Weiss with apologies, conducted him to
the door with a hand on his arm, and in turn was bid
goodbye not in resentment but affably.

'We shall not get a photograph through from Dublin
today,' Rodrigo said, motioning O'Malley to a chair. 'I
have been through to the Communications Secretary. I
am afraid the cable is snagged.'

'And the satellites are waterlogged.'

'Not unusual this time of year. Tonight I think you
will see your first Manila storm.'

'If we're still here.'

'Of course,' agreed Colonel Rodrigo.

Not only the Colonel but his matching office impressed O'Malley : the self-regarding shine of the Police
Chief's upholstered swivel chair, the chrome and steel,
the intercom, videophones, Telex, flowers, showcase of
pistols, panels of inexplicable switches, communicating
doors, plate glass and view over United Nations Avenue,
all this induced in the Superintendent a renewal of the
jealous pang which he had felt the previous evening,
arriving here to send his cable. The room was not perhaps so vast as an Irish Sweep director's, but it was four
times the size of his own attic in Dublin Castle, with its
table, two hard chairs, broken coatstand, and single-bar
electric radiator with the dent where Willie Connor,
semi-stotious one afternoon after the All-Ireland hurley
game, had trodden on it. O'Malley's eyes roved but
failed to locate the brown-paper package. Would the
paunchy officer telephoning at the far desk, he won-

dered, be Captain Taverna?

'You left Sergeant Maguire about ten-thirty outside the Hilton?'

'I did,' O'Malley said. 'Then he phoned the Tang fella, and brought the parcel round here. Or the other way about.'

'The other way about. He phoned Tang from here and left about eleven.'

'Two and a half hours ago.'

'There is nothing more you and I can do for the moment. Have you lunched?'

'Not yet.'

'You will do me the honour,' Colonel Rodrigo said. 'A working lunch. I promise you, any news of the Sergeant, we shall have it immediately.'

The *Los Olivos* restaurant stood in a side-turning leading to Roxas Boulevard, and though it seemed to O'Malley to be but a couple of hundred yards from police headquarters, they were chauffeured in the air-conditioned Buick. Inside, the restaurant was subfusc, without music, silent apart from murmuring voices and occasional chinking cutlery. A man in a black tie approached. O'Malley began reading the printed notice on the wall above his head.

*Pursuant to Ordinance No. 3820, possessors
of firearms and other dangerous weapons . . .*

The man in the black tie bowed to the Colonel and spoke to him by name. He led the way through an arch to an isolated table, and handed over menus.

'I want your Philippines Constabulary on this as well,'

O'Malley told the Colonel. 'I'm sorry, I'm not wanting to be alarmist, but if that boy doesn't show up in the next couple of hours, I don't say it'll do any good, but I'll be asking to see the President. Or as close to him as I can get.'

'The constabulary,' said the Colonel, 'is already informed. So is the Army. As for the President, if there is no word very soon I think he will be asking to see you. Forgive me, can we get the ordering out of the way? An apéritif?'

'Beer.'

The Colonel ordered a San Miguel, and for himself a Campari soda. For a main dish he recommended the Javanese sates, reaching across the table to point with a pearl-ringed manicured finger at O'Malley's menu. In spite of his clogged nose the Superintendent detected a sweetness from the patent-leather hair. The day was Friday, he remembered, and searching past the finger he found the fish and seafood section. He commanded fillet of lapu-lapu, whatever it might be, and whatever it might be he'd never taste it, not with this cold, and he wasn't interested anyway.

When the waiter had gathered the menus and gone, the Colonel said:

'I don't know how much you may have heard, O'Malley, or sensed, because I would have thought it was very obviously in the air, but there is going to be war in my country. With every respect to Sergeant Maguire, all the President needs is an international incident over an Irish policeman.'

'There'll be no incidents,' O'Malley said, 'so long as the lad shows up.'

'Exactly.'

'I mean alive.'

The Colonel emitted the faintest sigh. His fingers drummed on the table. He looked and sounded disappointed. 'Clearly,' he said, 'my own position has not occurred to you, and why should it? But you must understand that I survive by results. Results and politics. What do you suppose will happen to me if Sergeant Maguire does not show up – alive, and fit?'

O'Malley frowned, shook his head.

'The subject,' said the Colonel, flicking the subject away with a backhand gesture, 'is irrelevant and not to be discussed. I am certain the Sergeant is all right.'

'You didn't sound so on the phone.'

'One must set the wheels in motion. Have patience. If you are willing, I would prefer an account of your morning. All you have seen and done. Facts and impressions, both.'

'It doesn't come to much.'

'Who knows? Were you aware that Burke – ah, Byrne – did you know he has a bank account here totalling forty thousand dollars? That crumb I gathered this morning, for what it is worth. And at Camp Hay is an American officer who has paid out twice, if our information is correct, to have Byrne killed? If we pool what we have, maybe we shall begin moving towards results.'

'It's nearly two o'clock, my sergeant was to meet me at twelve,' said O'Malley. 'Right now the only result I'm interested in is Derry Maguire.'

CHAPTER XI

THE POLICEMEN'S shoes touched under the table, as shoes sometimes do. On the second occasion they touched, O'Malley retracted his feet, tucking them under his chair. Colonel Rodrigo shifted into a sideways posture, legs crossed outside the table. The tight khaki glimmered like two monstrous glow-worms in the restaurant's gloom.

'The pianist's name was Alejandro Roque, if it's any use to you,' the Colonel said. 'He shared a room with a tart on Pasay's east side, and he was there when we picked him up. That was directly after you phoned Taverna, so he cost us nothing in time and effort. The girl has disappeared, but unless you convince me she may have something to tell us, we shall not look very hard. Whether he was killed first, then his hand cut off, or the hand cut off before they ended it for him, we do not know. I have no doubt it can be established. Except for the blood the room was apparently in fair shape. No signs of a fight. Of course, if the hand is not his we shall have to start again. But it is. By now it should be confirmed. You would like me to phone through?'

O'Malley, doodling, grunted a No. He had taken out notebook and ballpoint to write the pianist's name for the record. Having progressed so far as the first three letters he discovered that he not only would not be able to spell the name, but that he had no great desire to try. One dead Filipino pianist, with a couple of Irish ballads in his repertoire. He set the A-l-e within a balloon, then

83

gave the balloon a stalk and leaf. Now, in a semi-circle round this whatever, he doodled a profile of a mouth, open and teeth-filled.

'Taverna suggests possibly it is a gang killing,' the Colonel said. 'They are not uncommon. Because he was a pianist they first lopped off a hand, and let him see it done. What do you think?'

'Makes no sense. Why send the hand to me?'

'Indeed, why?'

'I'd talked with him, asked questions. The hand's supposed to say go home. Wouldn't y'say?'

'That is my opinion. Perhaps the advice is good.'

'Damn sure it is.'

'You will take it?'

'I might. When Maguire shows up.'

'Of course.'

Colonel Rodrigo sipped from his glass. O'Malley, drinking ice-cold beer, felt a drip hit his thigh. Each time he lifted the glass a droplet formed by condensation fell either on his trousers or his shirtfront.

The Colonel said:

'I feel constantly guilty about the impression you must have of us. I would assure you we are not so incompetent as you must think. The phone situation is unfortunate. For some hours last week we were without communications to Australia, but in our storm season this is not unusual. Now you are anxious about Sergeant Maguire. I am confident you have no need, yet I feel guilty again. Tell me, is he ambitious? A little unorthodox?'

'What d'ye mean?'

'I have had men who have tried to make a spectacular coup on their own. They get an idea, or information, and suddenly they yearn to produce the rabbit from the hat, for glory, or promotion.'

'I know the sort.'

'And you know Sergeant Maguire better than I do. Possibly with an hour on his hands he has chosen to visit Byrne's apartment, or return to the Miami Club, or asked to see the constabulary's files. Something. Perhaps enterprise of this sort is to be encouraged.'

'There'd be two schools of thought on that.'

'Senator Cruz, for example. After the President probably our most influential public figure, and rather more approachable. He might be worth meeting. An *ilustrado*. That is to say, of our aristocracy. You know of him?'

'Opposition fellow?'

'This Byrne business must be tackled at the top, O'Malley, I am certain of it, among men like Cruz, and the Americans. Ewart Hart, obviously, were he in circulation. Let us be honest. Byrne has fed guns to the guerrillas. He consorts with their leader. No sooner is he in gaol than he walks out again, free. He is not on the fringes of this power struggle, he is there in the heart of it. The power is at the top of the heap, and if we are to know about Byrne it is at the top we should be asking questions.'

'Maguire would have let me know.'

'When I say Byrne has cash in the bank, I mean he had, up to today.' The Colonel swirled the pink fizz in his glass and drank. 'We have sequestered it. Is that the word? Not strictly within the law, but martial law offers a little extra scope. It will be for Byrne to prove the money is not payment for gun-running. Incidentally, you know Byrne? You have met him?'

'Years ago. I'd not say I know him.'

'Did he seem mad for money, for high living? I am trying to get a grasp of the man, to fathom him, but he is not a Filipino. We are an open, extrovert people, or we think we are. The big gesture, the noble deed. Our passion is for the primary colours. We do not smoulder, we blaze. When our senators signed the revised constitution, several signed in their own blood. There is no cunning in us. But Byrne, am I wrong in supposing he has cunning? Twenty-four hours after he walks out of Camp Crame, still we have no sign, not a whisper. If a Filipino escapes from gaol he heads for the market-place to beat his chest. Where does Byrne head for? Who are his friends? Is there a woman? We do not even know when he entered the Philippines. Probably two years ago at least. He has sung in public, for the Americans. He smuggled transistors from Japan and silver from Hong Kong, like many others. We know he was into the drug traffic in Palawan. So is he an adventurer or what? We must find him, O'Malley. But I cannot even guess at what goes on in his mind, which way he will jump.'

'You'd have to be a psychiatrist,' O'Malley said.

When the Colonel realized this was to be his guest's only contribution he tucked his napkin into his open-neck collar and picked up his soup spoon.

Relenting, O'Malley said : 'He seems to me the sort would chop off a man's hand.' His head bowed towards his soup-charged spoon. 'A fanatic for fanaticism's sake and the divil take the cause. I'd also hazard Camp Crame will have given him a scare. The Irish consul says he's in the hills with the Maoists. I don't know. Suddenly he's a felon again, fingerprinted from here to yonder, looking over his shoulder, pushed up against the wall by coppers' truncheons. I'd say he's deciding his

spell in the Philippines has run out, and he'll be scrap-
in' some loot together, and off. If he's not already gone.
You've got all your airports watched, harbours, all that?'

'Of course.' A brown drip of soup detonated on the
Colonel's napkin. In contrast to his fastidious appearance, he was a flamboyant eater. He had shredded his
bread-roll into his soup, and now the spoon splashed and
dripped. Soup slurped into the matinée-idol mouth. 'But
it would not be difficult to slip through. Ideally, for us,
that is what he will do. The further the better. Let some
other country worry.'

'So he's slipped through and sailed away,' said O'Malley, 'or he's in the hills, or gone to ground with his
wealthy pals, waiting for the private plane to fill up its
tanks. 'Tis a range of possibilities. At least you can count
on not findin' him in the market-place. Wouldn't your
best plan be the rich friends? Or enemies? The American
officer you mentioned, would his name be Ball? Or
Saunders?'

Colonel Rodrigo looked up from the soup. 'Good. As I
had hoped. Perhaps it takes an Irishman to catch an
Irishman. May I ask where you heard these names?'

'The consul.'

'In what context? You must tell me about this meeting. Does she know them?'

She? Who'd said, wondered O'Malley, the consul was
a she? He hadn't, and the impression he'd had from the
Police Chief was that he, the Colonel, hadn't been aware
of a consul's existence, male or female. But the Colonel
had supplied the phone number. He might have found
out about her. O'Malley blew his nose, unsure of himself, angry. If he'd reached a point of disbelieving everyone at the drop of a pronoun, as well pack it in. Apart

from the damage to the soul, suspicion left a man floundering in empty alleys, and useless.

'Gather she met them somewhere called Camp Hay,' he said.

'Where I,' said the Colonel, 'have spent all morning. Profitlessly.'

Not entirely profitlessly, he amended, and wiped the napkin across his soup chin. The John Hay Airbase was situated high among the pines at Baguio, the President's summer capital, and was supremely relaxing, given time to relax. O'Malley ought to go, lie in the sun. With Sergeant Maguire of course. He had met Major Saunders, but he had not wanted Saunders, he had wanted Ball, and according to Saunders, Ball was away on a week's pass. But according to a librarian he had met in the officers' lounge, Ball had been transferred to Clark Airbase. At the bar he had talked with a football coach who understood that Lieutenant Ball had returned to the States on compassionate grounds. When he had tried for a second interview with Major Saunders he was told the Major had left for Manila, something to do with a shipment of sports equipment.

'The librarian, the others, I think they did not know where Ball was,' said the Colonel. 'Major Saunders either knew and lied to me, or only pretended to know, and hadn't the least idea. I felt my presence embarrassed him.'

'You could check with whoever issues the passes.'

'Taverna has done so. Major Saunders issues the passes.'

Maguire is missing, Paddy Byrne is missing, and now, meditated O'Malley, this Lieutenant Ball is missing. 'Twas an infection, and spreading. He said: 'So what's this about Ball trying to have Byrne killed? If it's right, mightn't it be a notion to let him get on with it?'

'The constabulary picked up a hood two months ago. He had broken into Byrne's apartment at Philamlife, armed to the teeth. Revolvers, knives, everything. Unfortunately the constabulary were not interested in him, or the weapons, or the apartment being Byrne's. At that time they say they had never heard of Byrne. All that interested them was that the gunman had five hundred pesos on him.'

'Why?'

'Why were they interested? Pesos, my friend, are money.' The Colonel fell silent while a waiter cleared the soup plates. 'It was a profitable night for the constabulary.'

'Distributed?'

'Naturally. And the burglar, or assassin, if you like, was presumably distributed into the harbour. The question I thought you might ask was where did the money come from?'

Another pause for the ritual of the white wine. The wine-waiter pouring a taste, the Colonel sniffing, sipping, nodding assent. The wine-waiter pouring liberally, departing.

O'Malley said, 'You'll be after astonishing me but I'll say he filched it from Byrne's apartment. Supposing Byrne wasn't at home to stop him.'

'That was the assumption,' the Colonel said. 'Byrne wasn't home. But there is no record of Byrne reporting money stolen.'

'We said he's not one for the market-place.'

'This morning our informant tells us that Lieutenant Ball, recreation officer at Camp Hay, withdrew from his account, on the day of the burglary, five hundred pesos.' Colonel Rodrigo raised his black eyebrows, bared the white teeth in a smile. 'Coincidence?'

'Possibly. But I like your informant.'

'You have met him. Peter Tang.'

O'Malley nodded. Not wishing to disappoint the Colonel, he continued to nod solemnly. He was at a loss to see the significance, if there was significance. What surprised him was the absence in him of a sense of surprise, or even of real interest. Less than twenty-four hours in Manila, and the people he'd encountered were still anonymous, the names that had been named were mere words : a half-dozen disconnected facts rattling in a vacuum. If the President had been the informant, or the Papal Nuncio, or a bare-legged waitress in the Café Coquilla, he'd have felt equally unaffected. He glanced beyond the Colonel, through the archway, as though about to find Derry Maguire walking towards him, brief-case in hand, smoothing the moustache.

'We have confirmed Ball's withdrawal of five hundred pesos,' said the Colonel. 'Two weeks later Ball cashed securities worth three hundred dollars. That night Byrne's apartment was blown up.'

Just like home, O'Malley thought. He was expected to comment so he said, ' 'Twould have saved a deal of trouble if he'd been in it.'

'Well he wasn't. He moved into the Intercontinental, then took a new place in Philamlife. Bolts like girders and the full guard patrol. You are welcome to look it over, but the constabulary have been through it with steam-rollers. So, I confess, have I. If I might make a suggestion, a trip to Camp Hay might be more fruitful. And agreeable.'

'You think so.'

'One way or another,' and the Colonel gestured with upturned palm, as though hopeful of a tip, 'Byrne is involved with the Americans here. He is invited to sing to them. He has managed to steal their guns. Possibly this Major Saunders would talk to an Irishman. The truth is he is not enthusiastic about our own police.'

'We'll see,' O'Malley said, and looked at his watch. Two twenty-five. 'I'm not leaving Manila without my sergeant.'

A waiter arrived bearing tureens, and behind him the man in the black tie, who murmured to Colonel Rodrigo that there was a telephone call : Captain Taverna. Begging O'Malley's forgiveness, the Colonel stole away.

Lapu-lapu was in appearance not unlike haddock, or a swollen plaice. It came with rice, and on a sideplate a pallid, odourless vegetable that was outside O'Malley's experience. The Colonel was gone barely more than two minutes, yet even before he returned O'Malley knew that he would be eating no more lunch. He took a swallow of wine. The Colonel approached, his dapper shoes flashing and clicking like a dancer's across the tiled floor.

'The Hilton has been looking for you, they've had a package delivered,' he said, picking up his cap. 'In such a condition, evidently, they have taken it to headquarters.'

The policemen brushed past waiters and out of the *Los Olivos* gloom, leaving behind them a languishing lapu-lapu, sideplates, white wine, and a shrugging man in a black tie.

CHAPTER XII

THE PAUNCH of Captain Taverna sagged over the desk, stirring printed papers and a portion of chocolate bar, but keeping its distance from the red mess in the desk's centre.

'We've got the girl who delivered it.' Jowly, chewing, he stood with fists on hips, looking from the desk to the faces of Colonel Rodrigo and O'Malley, and back to the object on the desk. 'Says two guys in a car handed it her plus one peso, a block from the Hilton. That's the best you'll get from her. She's eight.'

The Captain had protected his desk with a copy of the *Chronicle* spread out. On the *Chronicle* reposed the paper wrappings and open box of a package not dissimilar to the one Sergeant Maguire had opened in the Café Coquilla. The most striking difference was that the pianist's hand had been modestly stained, while here was a lake of blood. Nauseated, O'Malley turned his head.

A patrolman was called to convey the *Chronicle* and its contents to the laboratory. Colonel Rodrigo, Captain Taverna and O'Malley trooped behind in silence; along corridors, down in an elevator. In the laboratory a man took photographs, a cheerful woman in a white coat produced tongs to separate the box and its wrappings from the hand. She set the former in a plastic bowl, and the hand in a kidney-basin. The policemen did not follow when she retired with these exhibits to a bench. An older woman joined her. The two white coats conferred like ice-cream salesmen over a new line in pistachio. They worked with bottles, brushes, powders.

'All you'll get from the girl is the car was white and the two guys friendly,' Captain Taverna said. 'Normal friendly guys like not big, not little, not young, not old, not thin, not fat. And they wore clothes.'

'Filipino?' the Colonel said.

'Right,' said the Captain.

O'Malley was aware of the glances they gave each other, and him. Faintly through his stuffed nostrils he could smell formaldehyde. He selected a metal cylinder from a selection of such cylinders in a rack at his elbow, and on removing the cork saw crystals like washing soda. He replaced the cork and cylinder. The two white coats approached, the younger carrying an enamel basin. In the basin was the hand, washed and hygienic inside a transparent bag. She gave the basin to the Colonel, who passed it to Captain Taverna.

'Male,' she said, 'aged between fifteen and fifty. Alive and kicking until, well, say two hours ago. I expect I don't mean kicking.'

'Not Filipino,' O'Malley said.

'Oh no,' she said, but offered nothing more specific.

'What, then?'

'I am not an anthropologist,' she said, and smiled. 'Caucasian, I imagine. Wouldn't you agree?'

'I'm not an anthropologist either,' said O'Malley.

He was conscious of the Colonel watching him, awaiting the sign of recognition, or rejection, but he could give neither. The hand was a hand: pale, large, decently kept nails, and a sprouting of hair on the back of the third joint of each finger. He could recall nothing of Maguire's hands. Had there been bitten nails, scars or rings, he would have remembered.

'Anyway, it is not Sergeant Maguire,' the Colonel

announced.

'How'd ye know?'

'It cannot be.' His tone was impatient. 'We have ten thousand white Americans in the Philippines, another thousand Europeans, why must it be Maguire? Why should it not be the Lieutenant Ball? How do we know he has not committed the supreme folly of finding Byrne? How do we know for certain it is Caucasian, why not Chinese? Age between fifteen and fifty, what help is that? Why not between ten and a hundred? We are wasting time.'

'Dr Virata will be in at five,' the older woman said coolly. 'He will give you a detailed report.'

'He will give it me now. Where is he?'

'He is not due until five.'

'Get him,' the Colonel told Captain Taverna.

The Captain proffered the basin to O'Malley, who put his hands in his pockets. Colonel Rodrigo snatched the basin and thrust it at the younger woman.

'Tag it,' he said, and turned on his heel.

Captain Taverna picked up a telephone. O'Malley followed the Colonel from the laboratory. I'd be in a state myself in his position, he thought. Demotion to the ranks for lack of results. Or the public execution. Or whatever.

By the time they regained the Colonel's office, the Chief of Police had collected himself. He ordered a check on all hospitals. He talked on the phone with the American military police. Graciously, almost touchingly, he apologized to two moustached men of Nordic colouring who had been led in for identification. Then he called for coffee and sandwiches.

'The Manila police are at your disposal,' he told O'Malley, and lit a cigarillo. 'I have an appointment at four-thirty with the Justice Secretary, otherwise I too am at your disposal. I do not know what you intend but you can meet Senator Cruz, if he is available. Or I can arrange a flight for you to Camp Hay. Captain Taverna will accompany you should you wish.'

'If I can borrow a phone I'll have another go at Dublin. And I want to see the President.'

The Colonel's hesitation was momentary. He blew a smoke-ring, motioned to a phone, and drew a second phone towards himself. 'If you try Dublin, I will try the President. Zero-nine gets you the central exchange. Mention my name.'

O'Malley dialled the number but did not mention the Colonel's name. A supervisor, female and solicitous, believed the circuit with Dublin might be restored by evening. O'Malley thanked her. He put down the phone, and listened mystified to the Colonel's dialogue with successive aides at Malacanang Palace. The conversation which had begun in English, then broken into what O'Malley suspected to be Spanish, was continuing in the implausible language which he had discovered to be Pilipino. A khaki policeman set down sandwiches and containers of coffee. There fell a hiatus in the dialogue during which Colonel Rodrigo wrapped ringed fingers round the mouthpiece and said to O'Malley, 'It is okay.' He uncovered the mouthpiece, spoke again in the language that was Pilipino, and hung up.

'Seven-thirty at the Palace. You should be there by seven-fifteen.'

'The President himself, or a minion?'

'The President. If you are here about seven we can go

together. Go alone if you prefer, naturally. It is very close. I can offer you a car.'

'Here at seven will be grand.'

'Excellent.' The Colonel ground out the cigarillo in a spotless ashtray. 'And meanwhile?'

'One or two things.' A bath for a start, O'Malley had decided, and simply to be alone to think. 'You'll let me know the second you hear anything.'

A covey of American tourists, fresh from the airport, were picking through baggage in the Hilton lobby. O'Malley walked round them in the direction of the reception desk. Either no one's told them, he thought, or they collect civil wars, like the one or two used to come roaming to Belfast and Londonderry.

Or no one's told them, was his second thought, because there's nothing to tell, and it's the Colonel's putting the wind up me so he can get me out and away before I'm dropped in the crossfire. Or before I find Byrne.

The last possibility brought a look of puzzlement into the grey eyes, because it was no manner of possibility. God, there was no sense to it at all. When thoughts of that class started up, it was a sure warning to stay out of the sun. The Colonel was a man of the law and honest as the day, wasn't he?

Was he?

The desk loomed. O'Malley worked at expunging the Colonel from his mind. He decided: If there's another package I'm having no part of it, it can go direct to the Colonel.

There was no package. O'Malley received his room key, stares from the clerks, and one message. The message, on a folded scrap of hotel notepaper plucked from his pigeon-hole, was addressed on the outside to *Mr Omaley*, 374. Inside, the round longhand advised: *Sultana Bar if you want burn.*

'Where did this come from?'

'I think,' said the clerk, scrutinizing the paper, 'it was a phone call.'

'When?'

'A moment.'

The clerk called to a girl pressing buttons on a calculator. She came forward smiling like peace and unity among nations, and glanced at the message. She had answered the call at about two-thirty, she thought. No, the man had said nothing more. Yes, a man's voice, American perhaps. Right, not long ago, half-twoish.

'Do you have a Sultana Bar?' O'Malley said.

'Take the escalator,' the clerk began to say, and O'Malley already was looking round the lobby, finding his bearings.

The Sultana Bar was closed, or if not closed, abandoned. The doors were open, but through them darkness and silence were almost total. Jolly painted characters on a board informed that at 5.30 commenced the Happy Hour, with drinks prices reduced by one-third. O'Malley ventured towards the sole glimmer of light, emanating from the bar. Behind the bar a man with pencil and paper and wearing toreador trousers and a spangled bolero was on his knees among bottles, stock-taking. He jumped to his feet and said:

'Sir?'

'Name's O'Malley. Would you know if anyone's been asking for me? O'Malley?'

'O'Malley. O'Malley. Who has been asking, sir?'

'That's what I'm saying, has anyone been asking? In

the last hour or so?'

'What sort of person, sir?'

'American possibly.'

'We have more Americans than you've had breakfasts. We're the Fifty-first state.'

'So there's been no one.'

'I didn't say that.'

O'Malley sorted out a banknote and placed it on the counter. The barman allowed it to rest.

'Olympia Massage on Roxas,' he said.

'What?'

'Massage outfit, other side the Hotel Filipinas, Roxas Boulevard.'

'He mentioned me?'

'He said if a man calling himself O'Malley arrives he's at the Olympia Massage.'

'I say if you're coddin' me you'll be on the street with your lovely waistcoat knotted round your neck.'

The barman met O'Malley's gaze, picked up the banknote, folded it, and placed it in a pocket of the bolero.

'All right so,' O'Malley said. 'How long ago?'

'Half an hour.'

'What did he look like?'

'Glasses, tartan jacket.'

'Would by any chance the name Byrne mean anything to you?' O'Malley paused, observing the barman. 'Or Burke?'

'Burke,' echoed the barman.

'Or Maguire?'

Obviously not, decided O'Malley. Without waiting for a reply he quit the Sultana Bar.

The American tourists in the lobby craned forward in a cluster, heeding the voice of a girl in a forage cap who lectured with her hands clasped in front of her as though in prayer. In the forecourt the doorman flagged a cab. The heat rose in ripples from the concrete. An earlier occupant of the cab had left orange peel on the back seat, and O'Malley brushed it aside. When the door was shut he leaned towards the driver. Embarrassed, he said :

'Olympia Massage, Roxas Boulevard.'

At a stop-light the taxi waited behind two army trucks filled with troops. The smooth faces of the soldiers looked half-awake, the muzzles of their carbines slanted towards the sky. Southwards along Roxas Boulevard, O'Malley looked at the ocean to his right, to his left the downtown glitter of hotel foyers, offices, casinos, shopping arcades. Above a cool glass entrance he glimpsed a Union Jack. Bicycles had been propped against a palm tree. When the taxi pulled in at the kerb he spied a neon sign : Olympia Health & Massage Parlor – Steam Bath – Japanese Sauna – 9 a.m. to Midnite.

He dug in a damp pocket for the fare. As he stepped from the cab a voice called, 'Hey, Joe, shoeshine?'

I don't know what happens in a massage parlor but it'll not be happening to me, not even in the line of duty, and that goes for the Japanese sauna, beating myself with chrysanthemums, and the steam bath, O'Malley promised himself, hurrying through a cascade of sunlight and into the Olympia.

He entered an effeminate salon that summoned images of the last days of the Roman Empire, or a fashionable hairdresser's. There was too much mosaic and lapis lazuli, too many damask cushions, and at opposite desks sat the only visible tenants of this part of the bordello, two beauty queens : two South Seas receptionists with eyes like black olives, one doing something mundane with glue and a glossy magazine, the other buffing her fingernails. Both looked up to smile at the new client.

Not even with these two either, O'Malley assured himself. Particularly not with these two either. When he spoke his voice was soft.

'Afternoon. Name's O'Malley. I was wondering, don't know if you can help at all, but could y'tell me perhaps, might you have a man in here, a customer possibly, askin' after me? O'Malley.'

'He left only a few minutes ago, sir. He was in a hurry. He said he'd be at the cemetery.'

Detective-Superintendent O'Malley took out his hand-kerchief and sponged his nose. The action bought time, and O'Malley needed time to think. Instead of thought came only, overwhelmingly, a sensation of humiliation, of being made a fool. Word had spread : the Irish jester was in town, the gas artist, the slapstick man with the red nose and shillelagh and copper's feet. Lead him on, feed him his own class of blarney, next stop the burying-ground.

'A Filipino?' O'Malley asked.

The beauty queens looked at each other. One said, 'American,' and the other nodded.

'Did he give a name?'

'No.'

'Wearing a jersey?'

Again the receptionists regarded each other, puzzled. The second receptionist said, 'One of those Scotch jackets, you know? Is it plaid?'

'Could you tell me how far's this cemetery?'

He was obliged to accept the establishment's card before bidding the beauties goodbye. At the kerbside,

prickly with the sun's heat, he raised an arm for a taxi.
A tan Chevrolet crawled past. Inside, looking out, sat a
quartet of American military policemen.

O'Malley's cab was a dilapidated Volkswagen without springs, air in the tyres, or seemingly oil, but with an
effective horn and astonishing brakes. Driven by a ber-
serk youth, it clattered southwards out of the city in a
succession of vigorous bursts, swervings and stallings,
and with a rattling exuberance that was not justified by
its speed. O'Malley wanted to promise himself that if ever
he reached the cemetery and the gravedigger told him
yes, the American in the tartan jacket had just left for
the beach, or the snake-farm, or wherever the next port
might be, then he would return to the Hilton, try Dublin
again, and the Colonel, and prepare himself for the President. But experience had taught him to promise nothing in advance. As well decide how to cope with the
next tennis serve before it came at you. A policeman
coped with situations as they arose. Or didn't cope. He
followed his nose. If Tartan Jacket was who he thought
he might be, with knowledge of Byrne, maybe with
something to say about Derry Maguire, he'd likely follow
until he found him.

The city retreated, the cab lurched through a desultory
landscape scarred by hoardings and shanties, unre-
deemed by the coconut palms with trunks like concrete
piping. *Island Cement. Cathay Pacific. Caltex. Global
Automotive Service.* Barefoot children swarmed in a
walled playground, on the wall the name Little Flower
Nursery School. Beyond the playground, tired allotments
of lettuce and tomatoes, and a grandfather in a coolie
hat, pails dangling from bamboo poles across his shoul-

ders, as in the smudged photographs of half-remembered
geography books. Scavengers picked with sticks through
a smouldering wasteland of garbage. O'Malley turned
his head from the garbage and saw on the other side of
the road a cemetery.

The cemetery lay at the centre of a rotting shanty
town; a white forest of crucifixes crushed and thrust
against from every point by the planks and corrugated-
iron roofs of the dwellings. The bleeding hearts, the
lurid madonnas with simpering lips and an arm aloft
in benison, hailed the Catholic Irishman as he bucketed
by in the cab.

'That was a cemetery!' O'Malley shouted at the
driver.

'On,' said the grinning driver, pointing onwards and
simultaneously swivelling in his seat to bestow on his
customer the full charm and confidence of his grin.

'Watch the road!' cried O'Malley.

The road swung away from the sea, the landscape
changed. The cab bumped up a hill fringed by mansions, then dipped into a wooded area. There was an
absence of ragged urchins, scavengers. The driver coaxed
the cab up another incline, into the sun. He accelerated
round a bend, shaving the paint from a sight-seeing
coach, then halted.

'Military cemetery,' he said, turning to grin at O'Malley.

There were no madonnas, no encroaching shacks, but
on the impeccable lawns which reached away to his
right, and in front of him for as far as he could see,
O'Malley looked out at hundreds upon hundreds of
marble crosses: anonymous, identical, accusing. Occasional trees and their pools of shade interrupted the

precision of the numberless rows. The only life he could see was a party of men and women with cameras and guide-books, leaving the cemetery for cars parked on the road ahead.

'Keep going, slow,' he said.

The taxi grumbled forward. O'Malley stared through the window, eyes searching the green and white panorama. The driver pulled out to pass the parked cars, and O'Malley turned his head, scanning the faces of the visitors with the cameras. The road curved. Fifty yards distant, among the crosses, a man was watching the road, shielding his eyes with both hands as he looked in the direction of the cab.

'Stop,' O'Malley told the driver.

The man in the cemetery wore a tartan jacket. Not for an instant taking his eyes off him, O'Malley delved for pesos for the driver.

CHAPTER XIII

SUPERINTENDENT O'MALLEY walked along a path between the crosses, and down a side path in the direction of the solitary waiting figure. Sunlight glinted on the man's glasses. Hands in jacket pockets, he made no attempt either to greet or retreat from the policeman. He was tall and angular with a stoop like an inquiring heron, and O'Malley wondered whether he was able to see, even with the glasses. The tartan drooped as though tailored for a broader man, or perhaps the wearer had lost weight. Only when within a half-dozen paces from the man did it occur to the Superintendent that one of the pocketed hands might hold a gun.

'O'Malley,' the man said.

'Lieutenant Ball?' said O'Malley, pronouncing 'lieutenant' with an 'f', the Irish way.

'On your own?'

'You saw the taxi leave.'

'You've got the Sergeant with you, haven't you?'

'He's somewhere else.'

'How'd you know who I am?'

'You're running away,' said O'Malley, who had not known, only guessed. 'Everywhere you go you get nervous and move on.'

'You'd be nervous, damn pigs dropping at you from one tree, Burke from another.'

'Byrne.'

'Sure.' Ball took from his pocket not a gun but a pack of cigarettes. As he spoke he looked about him, as though searching the trees for USAAF police, and Byrne. 'I'm running all right. *Adios* from here on, all the way. Tonight I'll be out of it. Gungy goddam country.'

'Out of it where?'

'Never mind where. I've got transport.'

He turned and walked along the path. O'Malley followed, cigarette smoke eddying back into his face. In the grass in front of each cross stood a miniature Stars and Stripes such as might be waved by an American child on the Fourth of July, or posted between the lectern and the Hush-Puppies on a Kiwanis luncheon table. Ball threw the cigarette away and turned to O'Malley.

'You're here for Burke, aren't you?'

'I am.'

'Try Cruz.' It was an order. Ball was walking again, hands in jacket pockets, O'Malley keeping pace. 'Har-

vard Avenue in Forbes Park. Six garages and an army
of guards. You might get in and you might not. You met
the noble senator yet?

'Heard the name. Byrne's with him?'

'If he's not, he's at Clark Airbase, or on his way. If
he's not at Clark, try Camp Hay. Or any place he thinks
he's going to find me.'

'Is it justice you're after, or revenge?'

'Right, all that, plus self-defence, plus I don't like the
colour of his neckties, I never did. None of your concern
what I'm after, O'Malley. Your job's to get Burke, I'm
telling you where to get him.

'Why not tell the police?'

'Police – here?' Ball halted on the edge of the path.
His head tilted back on the heron neck, his mouth
opened. No sound came out. The head jerked forward.
'That's rich, friend, that's truly rich. You know a name
then? You know someone is not on someone's payroll?'

'Believe I do.'

'Look, O'Malley, I know this country. I was here
when the POW's were flown in after Vietnam, that's a
life sentence ago. Police, constabulary, army, no difference, see? Every man jack on some politician's expense
account. And right now they're wetting their pants
switching politicians, they don't know which way to
jump. A cop I might have counted on yesterday, any
cop, today he'd put the dogs on me.'

'You think it's that close?'

'Listen, it's round the next corner. One more raid on
the Clark armoury and that's it. They don't even need
another but they're going to try. Why d'ya think Burke
was bought out of Camp Crame? Take my advice, get
Burke and get out.'

The cicadas sawed in the blue heat. O'Malley loosened his collar and wiped his neck with his handkerchief. Ball had halted again, looking about him, giving a longer look towards the only figures in sight, two distant matrons wandering among the graves. A car passed on the road.

'And don't try it on your own,' Ball said.

'I have my sergeant,' said O'Malley, his eyes on the American.

'Big deal. Just be sure you both take along an M-Six. Burke's partial to sergeants.'

'He's been blackmailing you,' O'Malley said.

'Smart ass,' said Ball, and slid a cigarette between his lips. 'Smart ass Mick cop.'

At Amiens Street Station, at Fatima Mansions and up Foley Street, outside the pubs at Charlemont Bridge on Friday nights and in the sodden early hours of Sunday mornings, O'Malley had heard himself more graphically described. Lieutenant Ball, he was certain, knew nothing of Maguire. All Lieutenant Ball knew was that he had to run, from Paddy Byrne, and from his own military police, and that he wanted Paddy Byrne kippered with an M-Six.

'Is Tang blackmailing you too?'

'Who?'

'Peter Tang. A Chinaman. Cement.'

'Never heard of him.'

O'Malley frowned at the engraved marble near his feet.

ROBERT T. PARKIN
PVT 127 INF 32 DIV
MARYLAND MAR 9, 1945

With few exceptions the graves were not anonymous. On all sides the roll-call reached away over the manicured grass, an al fresco catalogue of the dead. Herbison, Mundy, Zweigenthal, Foskett, Valenti, Lichocki, Leyden. From every State of the Union they had come to the Philippines. They were dated, tagged, identified. Some crosses bore the Star of David. One or two carried but a bare name.

JUAN SOLINA

Local boy, thought O'Malley, finds peace. Once in Normandy on an enterprising package tour, before fishing had gripped him and he had bid goodbye to enterprise, he had seen a similar greensward, a similar infinity of crosses. In history books he had seen similar cemeteries captioned Chattanooga, Vicksburg, Gettysburg.

He said, 'Ball, there's likely no sense telling you because to me you look beyond sense, but with or without your help Byrne's going to be caught, I'm not saying when, I'm not saying I'll be the one brings him in, but if you get back to camp and hand yourself over you'll live to hear all about it. I don't know whether you'll be hearing about it from inside a gaol, I don't know what devilment you've been up to, and if it takes a bit of the weight off your mind I'll tell you I don't bloody care, but from what I've learned about a thing or two, if you start trying to skip out, and if you think Byrne and his – '

'Take care of your own skin,' Ball said, thrusting his bony face close to O'Malley's. 'I know what I'm doing.'

Sunlight sparked on the glasses. O'Malley turned his

head and sneezed. He pulled a damp handkerchief from his pocket, dabbed eyes and nose, blinked.

HERE RESTS IN HONORED GLORY
A COMRADE IN ARMS
KNOWN BUT TO GOD

'You sure you're alone?' Ball was saying, his voice a semitone higher than earlier. The voice lifted still higher. 'They with you?'

Dabbing, O'Malley looked up, and seeing only a tree and the timeless filing-system of white marble, he looked first to his left, where two men were approaching along the path, then to his right, where a moment previously had stood Ball.

Now Ball was running. He ran with the ungainly flat-footed strides of a recreation officer whose speciality must have been charades and vingt-et-un rather than athletics. Though the legs were long the strides were short and uneven, like a first-time hurdler who has lost his step and seems at every moment about to trip. The shoes slapped on the concrete path, the tartan jacket billowed. O'Malley looked to his left. The two men, Filipinos, were running also, and there could be no disputing that both were harder, faster runners than Lieutenant Ball; or that they intended slowing to allow O'Malley time to remove himself from the path.

O'Malley side-stepped off the path and into sharp marble which dug into his hip. Off-balance, he twirled, clutched at air, and sat down. Waiting for the scorching in his hip to spread, or subside, and in these first instants after the collision there was no telling which would happen, he glanced up to see, or so he expected, the racing past of the Filipinos.

One raced past. The other veered off the path towards O'Malley.

The man wore black slacks, springy sneakers with soles like pork steaks, and a white open-neck shirt. He was of much the same square, bulky build as O'Malley, but fifteen years younger, and he carried his fists at waist-level with the intention of using them. One fist he had to unclench in order to grab OMalley by the arm and drag him up from the grass. The other he drew back like a hammer.

Unresisting, O'Malley allowed himself to be jerked forward. He could not have recalled when last he had been forced into a free-for-all. He knew only that he had not enjoyed them as a uniformed *garda*, when they had been routine, and that he had never learned to enjoy them. Now he dipped his head, and by digging his feet into the grass succeeded in accelerating the already considerable forward momentum imposed on him by the Filipino. The top of his skull thudded like a dud shell into the man's groin.

The manœuvre was unsubtle and effective, as it had been when O'Malley had discovered it in the sawdust bar of a pub in Rathmines. Then he had been twenty-two and on the receiving end. Now he smoothed his hair, placed a hand on his throbbing hip, and scanned the cemetery for Ball. The Filipino lay coiled on his side, foetus-like, the springy sneakers squirming backwards and forwards in an even tempo.

O'Malley set off at a run towards where Ball, thirty yards away, had deserted the path and was dashing across the grass for the road. Plainly he would never reach it. The comparison of the man in sneakers had so gained on him that he was almost close enough to bring him down, while diagonally towards the American from the road two more men were now in pursuit. Whichever direction Ball chose, he would be cut off. The tartan jacket swung and flapped as he zig-zagged between the crosses. One of the men running towards him from the road was jumping the crosses like a steeplechaser.

That the invaders were not police, American or Filipino, O'Malley had no doubt. Who they were he neither knew nor, for the moment, was about to consider. Excluding the sneakers man he had left behind, there were three, and they converged on Ball and fell on him when he was still a dozen yards from the road.

'Ball!' O'Malley shouted. He could not have explained why he shouted. He ran hard for the threshing bodies.

On the ground, kicking and struggling, Ball had dragged from his pocket not cigarettes but a pistol. He had taken hold of it by the barrel and hardly was it out in the air than it was swept from his hand. O'Malley clubbed with his fist the closest Filipino on the back of the head, then wrapped his arms round the arms of another. Apart from grunts and gasping the affray was as oddly soundless as it was brief, as though each participant had taken a vow of silence. Something O'Malley never saw collided with the side of his head and spread-eagled him.

When he looked up, Ball was on the ground, and one of the Filipinos was stabbing a knife into him with repeated rhythmic thrusts. The Lieutenant's mouth was open and dumb, his glasses were askew. The sun dazzled now on the glasses, now on the ten-inch length of steel.

The steel rose and fell.

'Ball,' said O'Malley.

For the second time the Superintendent never saw what or who struck him.

CHAPTER XIV

HANDS MANHANDLED O'Malley into the back of a car. Doors slammed, the car glided forward. He wondered whether his cold might be on the mend. The windows were wound up and there was no relief from the smell of sweat.

He was wedged between the character whose neck he had clubbed and a man wiping his hands with paper tissues. The first Filipino, whom he had laid low with his head, had recovered sufficiently to drive. Beside him in the front passenger seat sat a man in a pink silk shirt, the shirt slippery with sweat, who turned his head and said :

'O'Malley?'

'What?'

'Nothing,' the man said, but nodded in agreement, and handed back to O'Malley his wallet, warrant-card, notebook and passport.

The man turned front, and O'Malley leaned forward for a closer look at the photograph he was holding, which was of O'Malley himself, though not a print he recognized. It seemed like an enlargement from a staring passport photo taken ten years previously, when his hair had been black.

His head ached, and he could feel with his fingers the lump close to the crown. The hip ached too, but it was in

joint and functioning. O'Malley regretted that more
than anything, more than a sight of Derry Maguire, hale
and rosy and two-handed, or Colonel Rodrigo and a
division of police intercepting the car, or even a simple
hint of what in the name of God was going on, what he
would have liked was a mug of tea, and a bath. Banal
images of tea, soap and sensuous enveloping towels
lodged themselves with careful deliberation between the
Superintendent and reality. Events having been taken
out of his hands, he saw no sense in brooding or attempt-
ing to plan. The car had left the cemetery behind and
was driving through what appeared to be an army post :
green military trucks, field guns, a hundred khaki soldiers
on the grass doing nothing.

The car had also left behind Lieutenant Ball, un-
shriven among his long dead compatriots. Though temporary, his resting-place was probably as appropriate as
any. O'Malley let his eyes wander. The knife was nowhere to be seen. The man with the paper tissues was
ineffectually blotting the stains on his shirtfront.

Beyond the army the car crossed an intersection, then
drew up at a stop-light. A boy carrying newspapers and
a tray of chocolate bars, chewing-gum and cigarettes
ran to the car, and was waved away by the driver. The
car moved on, pulling out to overtake a horse-drawn cart
piled with bamboo. None of the four Filipinos was enthusiastic for conversation. The next occasion when the
car slowed, at a barrier manned by guards in blue uniforms, they turned their faces to be recognized.

The guards carried self-loading machine-pistols. The
barrier swung up, the guard nearest the car waved it
through, and as he did so spoke into a two-way radio.
O'Malley assumed he must be entering, through tower-

ing gates, a biological warfare research station at the least : top security, secret, as preciously defended as a sultan's daughter. The driver accelerated to thirty miles an hour, then slowed as the car approached a yellow-striped ridge built across the road. The car bumped over the ridge, accelerated, then slowed for the next ridge.

Avocado Road, Magnolia Road, Tamarino Road. The houses were sheltered by palms, eucalyptus, shaved hedges, livid flowering shrubs like preparations for a carnival, and here and there an immaculate white fence. Swept and dusted driveways led through prize-winning lawns to columned porticoes. Some houses sprouted col-onnades and wore cupolas like tipsy headgear, others were sprawling ranch-style constructions, their land-scaped grounds offering glimpses of clock golf, brick bar-becues, topiary, gardeners with powered grass-cutters. All, supposed O'Malley, had swimming pools, those pools he did not see merely having taken refuge behind the hibiscus groves and jacarandas. He was not, after all, in a cocooned research establishment, but in the bosky re-treat where lived the director of such an establishment, and his co-directors, with their wives and children, and their doctors, stockbrokers, architects, and possibly their bishop. These were not mere houses either, but resid-ences, or properties. Two guards stood by the driveway into which the car turned. They did not salute, but neither, O'Malley was happy to note, did they point their guns.

A gardener adjusting a water-sprinkler looked up to watch the car spurt past, then brake and halt. The low, spreading residence to which O'Malley had been brought was of the ranch-house group : timber and brick with outcroppings, first floor verandas where there existed first floors, and a main door of stained glass. The three passenger Filipinos alighted, leaving the driver to swivel about and say 'Out', though already O'Malley, beckoned by the man in the pink shirt, was half-way through the door. His guardians stood one on each side of him and one behind, in front of the stained glass, while the pink-shirted man pressed a bell, and the car moved away towards a garage with space enough for six Cadillacs and a small exhibition of motor launches.

A stocky flunkey opened the door. Instead of scraping and forelock-touching he stepped forward and opened O'Malley's jacket. O'Malley had a feeling he had been frisked during the lost moments following the knock on his head in the cemetery, but he was frisked again. The flunkey questioned, and was answered by the pink-shirted man, in either Spanish or Pilipino. The dialogue was monosyllabic: O'Malley, no polymath, failed to catch a single word. The escort-party accompanied him into a tiled hall hung with native masks and along a corridor that seemed to continue endlessly. Vigilant, tense when his manner suggested he was relaxed, even nonchalant, he was ready to run, or hit out, whatever might be required, the instant his guards relaxed their own vigilance.

But they did not relax. In front, the flunkey glanced back so frequently that he might have saved energy by walking backwards. At the Superintendent's side, the man he had clubbed in the cemetery kept a hand on his shoulder. A door was opened for him, and he stepped through on to a platform like a scaffold. Behind him he heard the door close, the key turn. More relieved than anxious, O'Malley found himself alone.

After trying the locked door, and listening to the re-

ceding footsteps, he descended three stairs into what appeared to be a storage room. Had the room been a cellar
it might have been a wine-cellar, for a generously stocked
winerack extended along the length of one wall; but the
barred window looked out on shrubs and split-level
lawns dressed up with rockeries, a pond, a sundial. The
door by the window, like the door through which he had
entered, was locked from outside.

O'Malley stood in the centre of the room and turned
slowly through three hundred and sixty degrees. The
room's contents included stacked deckchairs, folded tents,
tennis racquets, assorted lengths of timber, rolled carpet-
ing, cabin trunks and tea-chests. He poked among the
tea-chests: good quality glass and china, books, children's toys, mirrors, clocks, rejected oddments of orna-
ments in carved ivory and ebony. The books interested
him most. Though predominantly politics and Philippine
histories, there was also poetry and fiction. Examining a
selection of the books, he discovered on the flyleaf of
several the handwritten name Cruz: Joaquin Cruz,
Maria Cruz, Alvaro Cruz, Rafael Cruz. Where there
were greetings they were in Spanish, except in an instance where Alvaro had written, *Many Happy Returns
from Alvaro*.

The room was airless. O'Malley took off his jacket
and stood by the window, looking out. Either the gardeners had gone home or they were pruning elsewhere
in the grounds. He wondered how many incarcerated
heroes, in the books in the tea-chests, he might find
escaping from dungeons, castle turrets and locked rooms,
had he spare days for reading. His investigations of his
own prison revealed no way out.

None. Nowhere. O'Malley picked up and put down a

bone china teapot. He had no intention of smashing china, or the window, or shouting and banging, so giving the goons who'd brought him here the satisfaction of knowing he was in more of a state than he pretended. Likely as not he was being watched on some TV monitor. And if this were the pad of the Senator Cruz feller, he was not even sure he wanted to escape.

Judging by the class of some of the lumber, the owner might be enough of a Croesus to have paid for Paddy Byrne's exit out of Camp Crame.

O'Malley set up a deckchair, picked out a couple of lightish-looking books of verse, and plucked a bottle from the winerack. The label established the wine as French and almost certainly important. He'd have preferred a Guinness. He'd have given a quid for a pot of tea.

There being no corkscrew to hand, he used the pointed end of a tent-peg to force the cork cautiously downwards. The cork squeaked, all proceeding well until the final millimetre when it plunged like a depth-charge into the bottle and spurted red wine over O'Malley's hand, cuff and trousers. Wetly he settled back in the deckchair, drank, positioned the bottle on the floor beside him, and opened in the middle a book with faded covers entitled *archy and mehitabel*; by some boyo named, also in lower-case letters, don marquis.

> *and we sing*
> *and dance on the*
> *skylight to gehenna*
> *with the bourgeois*
> *bunch that locks*
> *their ice-boxes*

No knowing, mused O'Malley, sipping from the bottle, whether Cruz locks his ice-box. But he keeps a fair old cellar.

Cruz was no bourgeois though, he was aristocracy, if his information had been right. *Ilustrado*, that was the word, or something like. If you want Byrne, Burke, try Cruz, that's what Ball had said. Lieutenant Ball, USAAF retired. Why did Cruz not have a château or something if he was aristocracy. Château-bottled château.

O'Malley studied his watch : close on five o'clock, and through the window the sky was darkening. He held the bottle before his eyes, calculating that when the level reached the top of the label he would drink no more. All he knew he might be here through the night, watched on the telly. He'd no intention of getting himself cross-eyed, if that's what they hoped. Wasn't as though the stuff did anything for his thirst.

The book slid off his lap. His chief anxiety was that he would fall asleep and dream that he was up before the AC for falling asleep. Wine-drunk and asleep on duty. That'd be a dream he could live without.

Duty drunk and asleep on wine. Bottled on duty on château-drunk.

His head sagged, his eyes closed, he fell asleep, and slept dreamlessly.

'Up,' a voice said, and appended a second word that was foreign to O'Malley as it was, presumably, obscene.

The policeman took his time. For some minutes, perhaps for a half-hour, he had been between sleeping and waking. He had heard cars. He was unsure whether or not he had heard voices. From somewhere in the inner fastness of the Lazy Y ranch-house, Manila model, he had indisputably heard a clock chime. Now he opened his eyes to electric light. On the platform by the door stood the flunkey, the pink-shirted man, and Sneakers of the maimed groin.

'So you're coming or do we all take a nap?' the flunkey said.

O'Malley's muscles were stiff with sleep, his mouth was dry as gravel. Outside the uncurtained window he saw only blackness. He stood up and put on his jacket.

According to his watch the time was seven-ten. He picked up the bottle. The wine-level was as he remembered it, well above the label, and to wash the gravel from his mouth he took a perfunctory swallow. He stood the bottle on the floor and walked past the trunks and tea-chests and up the steps.

They proceeded fore and aft of him along the endless corridor, then a right-turn into and through a berugged and cushioned area that O'Malley did not recognize, through a library, and into what he supposed to be a living-room, or perhaps a senatorial study. The man writing hard at an oak table glanced up, beckoned prisoner and guard in, and carried on writing. O'Malley stepped sideways towards a semi-circular, sybaritic sofa in maroon leather, but before he could seat himself was forestalled by Pink Shirt intruding with agility between him and the sofa, and smiling like a hangman into his eyes.

He stood. The room was sumptuous, vast, and for his taste, impossible; a complex of so many turnings, openings, single steps, distant jalousies, louvres, screens, protrusions, painted handrails, shadows, and abrupt lakes of electric light, that there was no knowing whether it was

a room, or some intricate furnished lobby, or a half-
dozen rooms on a plan so open as to be without extremi-
ties anywhere. The man at the table banged a rubber
stamp on a document, pushed the papers aside, and
advanced briskly from behind the table. He said what
sounded to O'Malley like '*Vamos*', motioned the escort
from his presence, and with a smile and extended hand
approached.

He was in his thirties, podgy, and uninterestingly
dressed in white shirt, brown tie, slacks, and brown suède
shoes. O'Malley had supposed he might be a secretary.
His image of Senator Cruz was, or had been, of a man
tall, elderly, desiccated and illustrious. He held the
plump hand briefly. They sat facing one another on the
maroon leather, and the man said :

'My name is Cruz, I have some standing in our government here. I would like to welcome you to our country.' The voice was quiet, the words rapid, even rushed,
as though affairs of state pressed, and welcoming the
Ireland delegate was one of the least essential of these.
'Two things, Señor O'Malley. First, I apologize for any
inconvenience you may have suffered. I am sure you
understand. These men are loyal but totally without
tact. Second, and this falls a little ironically after my
most sincere welcome, I must advise you to leave the
Philippines.'

'With respect to the Philippines,' said O'Malley,
'there's nothing I'd like more.'

'Ah,' the Senator said brightly, as though problems
had been anticipated, and suddenly everything was
settled. He rose and strode towards a bureau. 'I mean
immediately, of course. Some day, in happier times, you
will visit us again.' He took keys from the bureau and

proceeded to a cabinet. 'Your flight is at twenty-three hundred, connecting at Hong Kong at, I believe, five-thirty tomorrow morning.'

'No chance,' said O'Malley, remaining seated.

'Don't worry, it is arranged, I have your ticket.'

'You can get a refund.'

Senator Cruz paused in the act of unlocking a drawer in the cabinet. 'I am sorry. You are saying you do not intend to leave?'

'Yes.'

'Do I have to ask why not?'

'By the speed of you jumpin' about you've not the time for questions.'

'It is you who have not the time, Señor O'Malley.' The Senator regarded his visitor with a look of pity. 'If you do not catch this flight you are unlikely to catch any other, ever.'

CHAPTER XV

A FIRST priority of Ewart Hart and his guerrilla army would be incontestably the airport, Senator Cruz explained.

Restored to his chair at the oak table, he had tinkled a brass bell shaped (very childishly, O'Malley thought) like a grenade, and now the flunkey loomed from a recess with a tray of bottles and glasses. Four hundred guerrillas had moved south from Bulacan, Cruz said. They were a day's march from Manila. A second battalion was advancing north from Batangas. The uprising was imminent. The President's army was demoralized. Half

were pretending to search the hills and praying they
would discover no one, the rest were biting their fingers
in Manila. Which way they would jump when the
moment came, only the moment would tell.

'Which way do you jump, sir?' O'Malley said, and
before he could be overwhelmed with a harangue on the
politics of revolt, added, 'If you're after sayin' I'm to
skedaddle for my own good before the shooting starts, I
say that's the daftest excuse ever I heard from someone
calling himself a politician. You don't give a tinker's
damn if I'm blown to bits. You're scared I'm going to
turn up Byrne.'

The Senator's mouth opened. He stood, a little pink
about the cheekbones, about to reply to the motion.
Beneath his feet the polished tiles reflected like water the
brown suède shoes. Before he could utter, O'Malley continued :

'Byrne, Burke, I'm taking him back to Dublin, and if
you're hiding him, I'm not saying you have him here,
but if you know where he's at you'd best deliver him up,
because I'll give you this free of charge, everyone here-
abouts seems to think you know.' He spoke without
pause, as rapidly as had the Senator, and more softly.
'What your purposes are I've no idea, and it'll likely
surprise you to learn I don't care, but I'd advise you not
to have Byrne murdered, like you had Lieutenant Ball
murdered. And that pianist from the Miami place. And
your hairy-scary phone calls, and nicking my telegram,
and dead hands in parcels. All that bloody rubbish. You
and Byrne are in all that together, I wouldn't wonder.
And what about these delays getting through to Dublin?
Is it you's clobbered the line, or is it cash you're paying
to the switchboards?'

The question was rhetorical. O'Malley did not pause
for an answer. The grey eyes never wavered from the
Senator's face.

'You're being talked about, sir, you've a name seems to
spring to people's lips, and unless you lean the right way
in this revolution, if there's going to be any revolution,
because it seems to me everyone talks and nothing happens, unless you've a following wind when the sparks
start flyin', I'd say you'll be having problems.'

Cruz opened again, then shut, his mouth. Momentar-
ily at a loss, he attempted an air of indifference, next of
amusement. O'Malley wondered to what extent senatorial leaders of the opposition were accustomed to being
put right by visiting coppers. He had not yet finished.

'Far as Sergeant Maguire's concerned, I'm fairly
hopeful you've not been stupid, because any unpleasantness there, you're starting very serious trouble. Sure you
know that, a personage of your eminence. 'Tis your
loyal houseboys I'm not so happy about. So whatever
your lark is I'm recommending you throw it in. Nothing
personal, sir, but if one hair of Derry Maguire is hurt I
personally shall see that you get broken in two. God
knows there's been enough messing about, and I'd like
Maguire back right now, if that's all right, sir, and
Byrne, and if y'don't mind, the loan of a car. You and
your bright lads with the knives have left me with –'
O'Malley tucked back his cuff, studied his watch – 'eight
minutes to catch an appointment.'

'Appointment,' said Cruz, surfacing, cued-in at last,
'with your wet-nurse Rodrigo?'

'Right so. Colonel Rodrigo, and the President.' Name-
dropping O'Malley reached towards the tray which had
been set down on a low bamboo table and snapped the

cap off a bottle of San Miguel. 'Himself.'

O'Malley's hands round bottle and tumbler shook
slightly as he poured the beer. He had but the haziest
insight into the character of the man across the shiny
tiled flooring, now sitting again at the oak table, dialling,
and pressing buttons which presumably would record the
conversation. Half the time he'd not been too positive
what he was telling Cruz, and some of the accusations
had met a blankness. Others, when the pink had risen
in the cheeks, had got home. If he'd pushed the Senator
too far there'd be repercussions right enough, likely in
the next moment or two. The loyal lads from the cemetery could not be far away. Judging by the shifting of
shadows beyond the archways and screens, the occasional chinkings and susurrations from unidentifiable
corners, they had never departed.

O'Malley drank from the tumbler, and felt the drip
of condensation drop on his fly. He watched the Senator. Speaking Spanish into the phone, the Senator
watched O'Malley. His conversation was brief. He replaced the receiver, pressed buttons, and said :

'Señor O'Malley, I confess for a moment I doubted
you, but you will concede that anyone making so many
ill-informed remarks as you must be suspect, even when
the facts may be correct.' He was up, striding to the
cabinet. 'Nevertheless, I apologize, it is true you were to
have talked with our President.' He took envelopes from
the cabinet and advanced on O'Malley. 'I cannot guess
what you hoped to learn from a traitor who knows
nothing, only betrayal and the techniques of brutal ty-
ranny, but in the event it is of no account.' He sat
plumply beside O'Malley. 'The only place you are
going, and I beg you to go quietly, as you policemen

are supposed to say, is home. These are your tickets.' He handed an envelope to O'Malley. 'Please, check them.'

O'Malley did so. There were two: first-class one-way flights via Hong Kong and London to Dublin, departing Manila International Airport, twenty-three hundred hours.

'One's made out for the Sergeant,' O'Malley said.

Senator Cruz said nothing, but passed to O'Malley a second, fatter envelope.

He says nothing, inferred O'Malley, either because it's all trickery, he knows Derry Maguire is dead, but a ticket for him implies that he doesn't know, that he knows nothing. Or he genuinely doesn't know, not even that the Sergeant was missing, and silence on the matter was *ilustrado* breeding, a refusal to rub home the falsity of the accusation. O'Malley was surprised to find himself believing the Senator knew nothing of Maguire's disappearance. He looked in the second envelope.

Jasus, I can buy the jetplane, he thought. He said, 'How much?'

'Count it, señor.' The Senator was smiling. 'With good wishes for your future in your own country.'

'More or less than you paid to shift Byrne out of prison?'

'Rather less, since you ask.'

It was the Senator's first admission. His smile had become fixed, like a pink strip of sticking-plaster. He stood up.

'I regret I cannot myself accompany you to the airport, but you will be in good hands. Your baggage will be waiting for you. There is no need to return to the Hilton.'

'Every man his price,' O'Malley said, handing the two

envelopes back to the Senator. 'Mine is Byrne.'

The hopeless smile declined to go. 'I can make things easy for you, señor, or hard.' Senator Cruz dropped the envelopes back into O'Malley's lap and was in motion again, striding to the table. 'You mentioned phoning Dublin, some difficulty. Your wife?'

'No.'

'It is important?'

'Yes.'

'The number?'

O'Malley told him, and the Senator spoke the sibilant Spanish into the phone. Waiting, holding the receiver, he said, 'When I am President, Señor O'Malley, our communications will be reorganized. Drastically. They will be second to none throughout Asia. We are not a poor country. There is huge potential.' Into the mouthpiece he said, '*Por favor. Si, si. Muchas gracias, señora,*' and hung up.

'Fifteen minutes,' he said.

The smile had become smug. O'Malley removed it by tossing both envelopes into a wicker waste-basket. Scooping a fistful of olives from the tray, he said :

'For a busy man you waste a terrible amount of time. I've told you, I'm in this country for Patrick Byrne. And I'll certainly not be leaving it without Sergeant Maguire.'

'I have never seen Sergeant Maguire!' Senator Cruz shouted, and slammed the palms of his hands on the table.

'You've probably never seen Ball but that didn't stop you!' O'Malley shouted back, advancing. 'Is Byrne so precious to you that everyone who doesn't think him so precious has to be killed or bribed the hell out of it?'

'Ball,' said the Senator, controlling himself sufficiently

to drop his voice, 'was a nuisance.' The fleshy cheeks blushed like a girl's. 'Like you, señor.'

The table separated them. Cruz and O'Malley glared at each other. Then the Senator shook the grenade bell, turned, and walked fast past the bureau, up a step, and out of the room.

As all alternative routes from the room might lead into God knew what blind alleys, O'Malley crossed to what he hoped would be a window. With a snap he released the blind. Phone calls to Dublin, if there genuinely was a phone call, which he doubted, would have to wait. His left hand, he discovered, was filled with olives. He threw them to the floor and began twisting knobs to unlock the window. When steps sounded close behind him he turned swiftly.

He was not swift enough to avoid approaching knuckles. They belonged to Sneakers and struck him on the side of the head. Almost simultaneously something solid, perhaps a knee, contacted his belly, and O'Malley knew that the fight, even before it had started, was over for him. He recognized a pink shirt and three or four familiar faces in vague proximity. Sneakers hit him twice more before he pitched to the floor.

Gradually through a turmoil of shrillings and buzzings the sound in O'Malley's head became identifiable as a telephone bell; and when the bell's ringing ceased, the vibrations seemed to continue. Under his cheek the cold tile was comforting. A few inches from his eyes he could see the smear of a trodden olive; and beyond the smear, beneath a fashionable three-inch trouser turn-up, a sneaker.

O'Malley raised and turned his head. Senator Cruz was replacing the telephone receiver with one hand, with the other jotting a note on a scrap of paper. He put down the pen and regarded O'Malley.

'You are ready now for your flight, señor?'

'Thanks all the same.' O'Malley closed his eyes. He made no effort to get up.

One of the houseboys muttered incomprehensibly. After a pause, the Senator said :

'A pity. I had not wished to leave you to these gentlemen. But I can spare you no more time myself. I have a hundred matters to attend to.' He appeared to have said all he had to say, but after a brief silence added, 'For example, that was a policeman acquaintance, on the phone. A report that Byrne is here in Forbes Park. Not at this address, you may be surprised to learn, but only a minute away. Of course there is probably no truth in it, but you see, already I have spent far too much – '

Time, O'Malley supposed the next word was to have been, but the phone interrupted. The Senator picked it up, listened, then removed the handset from his ear and held it towards O'Malley.

'Dublin.'

O'Malley clambered to his feet. With two strides he reached the table. He grabbed the phone.

'Hullo. O'Malley here. Who's that?'

'Sergeant Dempsey here, sir.' The voice carried to O'Malley with a faint echo from the far side of the world. It was indeed Dempsey; unexcited, in control. 'Grand to hear you sir, because the Assistant Com – '

'Sergeant, listen. Will you put me through to him. If there's the least delay get me Inspector Connor.'

Fingers descended upon the phone, cutting the connection.

'I will get you Inspector Connor,' said Senator Cruz,

'if you agree –'

The Senator howled as O'Malley brought the handset down on the podgy fingers. Before the policeman could lift the handset, or contemplate what next he might do with it, once lifted, a hairy forearm clamped round his neck.

Struggling, still holding the phone, he found himself dragged backwards. His heels became airborne. Senator Cruz was yelping and shouting. For fear that now he might glimpse the knife, O'Malley shut his eyes. Rustling, croaking sounds issued from his windpipe. He heard the telephone crash to the tiles, then nothing more as night and pain closed like a shutter over his head.

He felt alone and hoped please God that he was.

He believed he was alive. For the present, better alone than alive, and if that class of thinking were a sin he'd remember to confess it, next confession.

From somewhere there sounded continuous rumblings, as though the ocean had entered his ears, or furniture were being moved in an overhead room, but there were no voices, and for that relief much thanks. He was a Detective-Superintendent, he was sure of it, and he wanted no one looking at him in this state.

What was it the steeplechase jockeys said about spills? If you could get up and you didn't rattle you were all right?

He found he was able to sit up. He had both hands, Hail Mary full of grace. He could feel his hands on the tiles as he propped himself against the maroon sofa.

The lights were on. For company, on the floor, were stranded olives, and the telephone on its side, cracked and splintered. One sleeve of his jacket dangled from

threads, but he found in the inner pocket his wallet, and
Colonel Rodrigo's card. On all fours he progressed towards the phone.

The effort of dialling was great, and moments passed
before he realized the phone was defunct. He supported
himself on an elbow, gazing at the waste-basket. The
envelopes had gone. He looked at the watch on his wrist,
but it was smashed.

With new vigour the faraway rumbling broke out.
O'Malley wondered: the rebellion, is it begun?

On buckling legs, he stood. He took a long swallow
from the tumbler of flat beer, gathered from the table the
Senator's jotted note – 8, *Flame Tree Road* was all it
said – and stumbled to the window. No one, this time,
interfered with his turning of the locks.

No one interfered at any stage. Outside, the grass was
dewy under his feet. The first car in the garage had no
key. The second did have, and with the engine running,
O'Malley sat for a full minute in the driving-seat, eyes
wandering in search of a gear-lever, before comprehend-
ing that there was no gear-lever.

Either the guards slept or they had gone to the rebellion. O'Malley backed over flower-beds and drove into
Harvard Avenue.

Magsaysay Road. Mahogany Road. Narra Avenue.

If Flame Tree Road was but a minute away, already
he must have come too far. A U-turn. Foot down. An
exploratory turn, tyres protesting, into Mahogany.

O'Malley sat abruptly upright, shuddering, having
found himself driving with his forehead resting on the
wheel, eyes shut. The headlights illuminated a white
sign: Flame Tree Road.

A wrought-iron figure eight wired to a coconut palm

identified the house he sought. O'Malley braked and swung the wheel. At ten miles an hour the off-side wing struck the trunk of the palm, the engine died. Swearing, fumbling, the driver failed to locate the ignition. He weaved up the drive on foot, jacket sleeve dangling.

If Byrne were here? And maybe the Senator with him, and the houseboys? As insistently as the questions and their implications presented themselves, O'Malley rejected them. In his present undistinguished state, brain and limb, God but they'd only have to puff, he'd be down and out.

The rumbling was thunder, which sounded now from the direction of the sea, but more faintly than before. There was a dampness in the hot night. O'Malley leaned against the bell by the front door, sank to his knees, and passed out.

CHAPTER XVI

THE DIN was even more painful than on a dimly-remembered earlier occasion. The volume of the guitars, drums and voices of the four fresh-faced lads, as dated and nostalgic as flower-power, as the decade-old contests between Arkle and Mill House, had been lifted to the limit by a mad invisible recording-engineer. The crowd bayed, shots were being fired, and Paddy Byrne, in this episode not singing but fleeing, fled fleet of foot in running-shoes and dinner-jacket towards a building that burned like a panchromatic Reichstag, like the British Embassy in Merrion Square. In pursuit, in spite of every exertion, O'Malley ploughed through glue, progressing not so much as an inch through the mob. Brown hands pressed him back. The flames boomed in his ears.

'Byrne!' he cried out.

'Always Byrne,' said a voice, impatient and female, and O'Malley, floundering into consciousness, was aware of hands, one feather-light on his face, another sliding across his stomach and between his legs.

They were not his hands. One of his own hands reposed on a nippled protuberance that was not his either, being hillocky and devoid of hair. The other hand he could not immediately locate, but wherever it was it was abnormally warm. The nails of the foreign hand that had touched his face were now tracing parallel tracks down, then up, his flank, eliciting sensations that were either soothing or unnerving, he had not yet decided which. He opened his eyes, blinked into the eyes of the Irish honorary consul, and on closing his eyes felt the heat of her breath, and his eyelids kissed.

He had glimpsed a dawn greyness at the edge of the curtains. Thunder boomed distantly. Closer to hand clattered a chorus of birds.

'Is this Eight, Flame Tree Road?' O'Malley said.

It was the best he could manage. Sleep-filled, increasingly aware of the aches throughout his body, he had rejected other introductory remarks and been on the brink of saying, 'I arrest you in the name of the law,' words which after thirty years a *garda* and numberless arrests he had never yet said or heard said.

'Go to sleep,' whispered the consul.

'Is it, then?'

'Yes. You are hurt, go to sleep.'

O'Malley thought he would not. He extricated his too-warm hand, unmeshed his legs from hers, and sat

upright in bed. The covering fell away, and he reached
out and pulled it back over his lap. His aches opened
and groaned.

'And Byrne's not here?'

'No.'

'And never was?'

'Of course not. Lie down. If you will not sleep we will
make love gently, as before.'

'Don't be troublesome, woman,' O'Malley said, and
stared directly in front of him towards a feminine dressing-table against the wall. But he had to ask, 'Before?'

She drew the covering off his legs. 'You are a sensuous man. Very able. Considering.'

Considering, was it? Confused, sensing mockery,
O'Malley jerked the blanket over his legs and round his
waist. Devil take the woman. Likely she'd meant 'con-
siderate'. Not that he believed one word from her harlot's
lips. He glanced down, but she was looking up at him,
and he turned his eyes quickly from the brown small
breasts nudging his hip, the tumbled hair spread like
smoke on the pillow. His watch, he remembered, had
been smashed. Now it was no longer even on his wrist.

'What's the time?'

'I don't know,' said the consul. 'Make love to me.'

'Is Senator Cruz here?'

'Questions. Why would he be?'

'What about his houseboys? Don't be telling me 'twas
you lifted me into bed.'

'You remember nothing?'

'I remember you. Moral Sciences. D'ye mind me askin'
what a moral, scientific lady like you's doing in the
honorary consul business?'

'Always the questions. Even here, with me, you are

the policeman.'

' 'Tis a grim outlook. Was it Byrne got you the job?'

'No.'

'How about Tang?'

He glanced down in time to see her frowning, and substituting a look of appeal.

'Please, we will make love.'

'Where are my clothes?'

'Incinerated.'

Her tone was impatient again, defiant. O'Malley swung his legs on to the ice-blue carpet, stripped the covering from the bed, and draped it round him like a toga. When he stood, the noblest Roman of them all, aches reawakened in him, and to keep from falling he had to plant his feet apart. The dizziness passed. He found a light by the door and switched it on.

'We'll see about that,' he said, bending, searching under the bed.

He opened cupboard doors, the door into a bathroom, the door giving on to a landing where stood other doors, and stairs with a curling, descending banister. He stalked back through the bedroom, past the supine nude, and wrenched the curtains apart. The sky over the trees and rooftops of Forbes Park was spread out like a grimy towel.

'I'm borrowing your shower, if you've no objection. If I've no clothes by the time I've done I'll be phoning Colonel Rodrigo. And if you're not sure what I'm on about, he's your Chief of Police.'

I'll be phoning him anyway, he thought, and if there's delays on the line I'll be having the loan of another car. She watched him from the bed, in silence, like the coloured cover of a girlie magazine, maturer-woman edition. In the bathroom O'Malley turned on the shower and dropped the toga. Remembering too late to bolt the door, he found the way to the door blocked by the consul : princess-sized, cinnamon hands on his chest, and insinuating down his sides, over his hips.

'Look at yourself.' She raised her voice above the drumming of the shower. 'You need sleep, and care.'

'You try too hard. Out.'

In the moment of hesitation, pondering where and how to lay hold in order to eject her, he lost her. She sidled past, over the wall of the bath, and under the shower, where she squeaked because the water was too hot, or too cold. O'Malley wondered if her aim was to provoke him to violence. Or were there concealed cameras, eager for horseplay? Horseplay, whoresplay, the devil with you, thought O'Malley, looking in the mirror.

The busiest welt ran diagonally from ear to chin, but there were other lesser alarms. His left eye was partially closed, his lip swollen. There were cuts on the back of one wrist. His body was mottled with bruises of different hues. He found without asking a diminutive safety-razor and began to shave.

'If you leave here you will be killed,' she shouted from the shower. 'Burke will kill you.'

'Byrne,' shouted O'Malley, and nicked his cheek. 'You know a lot about it.'

'Stay here with me.'

'Where is Inspector Gwire?'

'Who?'

'Sergeant Maguire.'

'I have never seen him. If you will not stay, let me drive you to the airport.'

'You're a conscientious consul.'

'There is a flight at noon.'

'And an envelope of cash?'

'How much do you ask?'

'You're the investment person. How much am I worth?'

'Five.'

'Not at all, 'tis a sellers' market. Buoyant as blazes.'

'Seven.'

'God, that's too buoyant by half. Shall we forget the investments? Tell you what, I'll settle for my sergeant.'

'I know nothing about your sergeant!'

'And Patrick Byrne.'

'You are so stupid! Stupid, smug, incorruptible frog!'

Her cool having dissolved in the billowing vapour of the shower, she snatched a robe and strode from the bathroom, slamming the door. Almost cheerfully, victorious for the first time in thirty-six hours in Manila, O'Malley stepped under the shower. When he returned to the bedroom, a towel round his waist, the consul was seated at the dressing-table, selecting jewellery for her hair. She wore a green blouse, belt, and a crêpe skirt printed with entangled hoops which made O'Malley think of the Olympic Games. He said:

'My clothes?'

'Over there.'

They were a crumpled mess but they were there, on the bed; and in the jacket pocket, passport, wallet, note-book, warrant-card were intact. O'Malley started to dress. The consul, frosty-faced, was brushing her hair. The Antony and Cleopatra interlude was clearly over.

'Would y'mind telling me,' O'Malley said, 'why the Senator's so desperate to have me out of it? Is it the guns? If I remove Byrne, he's the only source for the guns Cruz buys and passes to the guerrillas, would that be it?'

'You know nothing.'

But I'm learning, I'm beginning to guess right, and you're frightened, surmised O'Malley. Observing the consul in the mirror, the pinkness that had entered her cheeks, he said:

'Ball, the American, he was being blackmailed by Byrne, he'd reached the point where the worm turns, so he had to be dealt with. By Byrne's orders or the Senator's?'

She brushed, frostily glowering.

'No matter, 'tis a detail,' O'Malley said, buttoning the stained shirt. 'What's intriguing now, is the Senator's hold over you.'

'Stupid. What hold?'

'I can see he'd not want me dead, my hands off and a stake through my heart and all that, because if it got out he'd anything to do with it, and likely someone'd be saying something, there'd be a fine old rumpus. So he tries to send me packing by the harassing and cajoling and bribing and threatening and of course a demonstration with the muscle. And now you. Clean sheets and love. A night of passion for the Mick copper, with promises of more to come, I'd not wonder. Is Senator Cruz your husband or your pimp?'

Silence.

'Well?'

'You disgust me.'

'He's your husband.'

'I am a widow.'

'But you sleep with the Senator. And for him, if he thinks it'll work, you'll clear a space in your bed for me.'

She swung round to face O'Malley, black eyes sparkling, hairbrush poised as if about to fling it. O'Malley, watching her, was on one knee like a suitor, tying a shoelace.

'You're lovers, isn't that so?'

'He is my brother.'

'Ah.'

Greater love hath no man than to lay down his sister for his country.

'He is my brother and the one man, the only man, who will save this country. You cannot understand, Irishman. Brother or whoever, what does it matter? For him, yes, I will sleep even with you.'

'I see.'

'You see nothing. What do you know! But you will see, very soon, when my brother is President. Or rather, you will not see. You will be dead.'

'Where's your phone?'

'There is no phone that you will find.' She swung round to face the mirror, and drawing her hair together at the nape of her neck, clamped into it an amber brooch. 'Not before you are collected.'

Collected? O'Malley moved to the window and looked down on the lawns and shrubs. He saw the drive where it decanted into Flame Tree Road, but no sign of his borrowed car. The treetops were silhouettes against the whitening sky.

He said: 'Have you been phoning?'

While I was under the shower? He pulled on the jacket with the dangling sleeve. Uncommunicative, the consul was sifting through rings. O'Malley hurried past her, on to the landing. He opened the door into the adjacent room.

He was looking at another bedroom, with no visible phone. So far as his glances were able to tell him there was no phone in the next bedroom either. Aware of aches throughout his body, he ran down the curving stairs into the hall, eyes searching the walls for wires, the hall tables for telephones. In a living-room he looked at an awakened cat, a stereo, books, piled magazines, wines on a bamboo bar, but no phone.

Devil take her. A woman like her, investments, Senator's sister, she'd have a dozen phones. Where'd she stowed 'em?

He hauled himself back up the stairs and into the bedroom. 'I'm tellin' you — '

The bedroom was empty. He looked in the bathroom. No one. To be sure the consul's telephoning had not yet produced results he crossed the bedroom and looked out of the window. A car, American, polished as a salesman's smile, was turning into the drive.

He ran from the bedroom, along the landing, three at a time down the stairs, and across the hall to the front door. Though closed, the door was unlocked. O'Malley applied bolt and chain, and ran into the living-room. The cat arched itself and surveyed him. Through a window O'Malley watched Sneakers, Pink-Shirt, Flunkey, and three others whom he did not recognize, scramble out of the car and advance to the front door.

He dodged round furniture and across the living-room to a pair of double doors which opened into a broad passage hung with paintings, and a choice of proceeding either to left or right. Behind him he heard muted rattlings at the front door, and footsteps on gravel.

He chose right, opened the first door he came to, and dashed through a kitchen towards the oblong window above the sink. The view was of empty lawns at the rear of the house. O'Malley climbed into the sink, fiddled with window-catches, and performed his second successful defenestration of the night.

Except that now it was morning. The sky was milky-grey, the dawn chorus of birds had given place to traffic sounds on some not too distant road. O'Malley listened for noises of footsteps and Filipino chatter approaching from the front of the house, but heard neither. Again he had a choice of right or left, or straight ahead through cosy bushes and into cover. But straight ahead promised poorly for transport. Sounds of voices somewhere behind and to his left settled the question. He turned right and pounded with accelerating speed along the rear wall of the house. No one was in sight until he came to the corner, where he collided with a figure who emerged with equal velocity from round the right-angled brick bend.

Amid mutual cries of shock the pair went down in a sprawl of limbs.

'Sir,' panted the felled, moustached figure, ' 'tis me, is it you?'

' 'Tis you, 'course it's me, dammit man,' O'Malley cried, gripping and squeezing the Sergeant's wrists and hands as though they were some amazing, unheard-of anatomical feature, 'where in God's name have ye been?'

CHAPTER XVII

THEY RACED across thirty yards of dewy lawn towards a barrage of azaleas. A shout carried from the house as they tumbled out of sight behind the bushes.

'Are we seen?'

'Not yet.' Maguire, prone on grass, peered through azalea trunks. 'Three of them, they're studying a window. Here comes another.'

'I can see,' O'Malley said, watching Pink-Shirt run round the side of the house, a pistol in his hand. 'Come on.'

They crawled backwards on hands and knees, keeping the azaleas between themselves and the house. They reached more azaleas and crouched behind them.

'Who's the woman, then?' Maguire said.

'Where?'

'There, on the right. Keep your head down. Sir.'

'That, lad, is the Irish honorary consul.'

'Is she, begob. The fellas, they were at a politician Senator's house. He's called Cruz. I'd just got there when they came breezing out, so I followed after, but I didn't see Byrne. One of that lot might be the Senator.'

'He's not though, he's the indoor type.'

'You've met him?'

'I've met everyone. Did they spot you?'

'Not sure. I thought just now they had, thought they were chasing after me. Maybe they were after you.'

'Have you a car?'

'Taxi.'

'Is it waiting?'

'Should be. I've not paid him yet.'

'There's no getting to it that way. Can we reach those hollyhock things, there?'

Further back, beyond exposed orchid beds, grew a hefty clump of tropical flora. They were not hollyhocks but poinciana, and a solitary cream frangipani. O'Malley and Maguire cautiously retreated, shielded by bushes. They dashed the last few yards to the new cover, and on gaining it, the nimbler Sergeant in the lead, heard a shout from the house.

O'Malley cursed. Craning round foliage, the policemen saw houseboys sounding the advance across the lawn. Sneakers had started to run.

'We're not playing hide-and-seek,' O'Malley said. 'Off, lad, fast as you like.'

Abandoning the flora, the policemen turned and sprinted. Cries and houseboys pursued them. Leading his chief, pacing him, Maguire plunged through a hedge, skirted a sunken garden, and charged through waist-high cogan grass. O'Malley galloped stiff-legged and breathless at his heels. They passed into and through other gardens, boots thudding, mouths gasping. When white ranch-style buildings swung into view, and Maguire slowed, uncertain whether these might be haven, O'Malley overtook him, veering away from the house and on to its driveway. They careered along asphalt, across a deserted avenue, and into a decorous copse of pink trees. Here, halting at last, they looked back. There was no one, as from the absence of shouting they had assumed. A car with two men inside went by, braking as it drove over a striped ridge. Early gardeners, O'Malley supposed.

We lost 'em the other side of the house, he thought, and said : 'Hold on, I'm destroyed.'

'You went like the wind, sir.' Panting, Maguire regarded his Chief. 'You've a range of lumps on you.'

'That's the Senator and his staff,' said O'Malley, and looking about him selected a patch of leaf-mould from where he could see the avenue without being seen. He collapsed on it and gulped air. 'Now!' His torso rose and fell. 'Where, if y'can summon the cheek to tell me, have y'been?'

'Think it's called the Tondo, sir.'

'The Tondo. A shopping precinct?'

'There are no shops in the Tondo, sir. 'Tis a dockside slum, what I saw of it. Shanties and vermin.'

'Who were they?'

'There were six in all, working shifts. Never a hope of getting out. They'd got guns, though they never waved 'em around. I'd a room like an airing-cupboard with the thermostat broken. They had the big room, and that was hotter. They spent the whole time cock-fighting.'

O'Malley paused in the act of raising a pink branch. 'Y'mean cocks like chickens?'

'They'd let me out into their room every hour or so, just to breathe, and it was filled with feathers, like a gale blowin' through a pillow factory. They clip these spikes round the birds' legs, sort of spurs—'

'Some other time, lad.' A paisley green and yellow butterfly flapped past the Superintendent's nose. 'So how come you're here?'

'I was looking for you.'

'I gathered that. I mean did ye loose the cocks on them, or did they tell you to run along now, or what?'

'That's the weird bit. I was in this cupboard, eating,

they kept bringing beer and hamburgers, and there wasn't this squawking and yelling any more. I fancied it must be the night siesta. I'd slept quite a bit myself, on and off. Anyway, they'd always locked the cupboard, but when I tried the handle it wasn't locked. The big room was empty, except for feathers. I just walked out.'

'Like Byrne out of Camp Crame.'

'I thought of that.'

'No one bought you out, lad. Something changed their minds about holding you, or they only wanted you out of the way for – how long was it?'

'Just under eighteen hours.'

'Long as that?'

'I was thinking it was a spot more of the harassment.'

'What did they say?'

'Nothing, nothing at all. I tried asking questions but all I got was to shut up and I'd be all right.'

'No muscle?'

'None.'

'How'd they get you?'

'I'd phoned Tang and fixed up for lunch, and I'd left the pianist's hand with Captain Taverna, then someone barged into me on the pavement. Next thing I was in the back of a car ragin' along like the wrath of God.'

'Incidentally,' O'Malley said, 'we've acquired a second hand.'

'Jesus, we have? Whose?'

'They're working on it.' For reassurance and the umpteenth time O'Malley caught himself looking at the big functioning hands of the Sergeant, one fooling with a pink blossom, the other stroking the moustache. The skin below the ends of the moustache, and the chin, bristled for want of a shave.

'So when did you walk out?'

Looking at his watch, Maguire said, 'Hour and a half ago, and after that cupboard you never smelled air so good, even in the Tondo. Took me fifteen minutes to get clear and find a phone-box. I phoned the Hilton but you weren't there. They said you hadn't been back, and kept askin' who I was and where I was calling from.'

'How did you find me?'

'I was going back to the Hilton, see if you'd left word, but I'd got Tang's card so I phoned him first.'

'That boyo. He's into everything. Why didn't y'phone the police?'

'The police?'

'Aye. Heard of the police? Colonel Rodrigo, he's one of them.'

The butterfly returned, perched on a leaf, and folded its two wings into one. When Maguire failed to answer, O'Malley grew cross. Mother of God preserve me from the sensitive, he prayed, and looked at the Sergeant. He found himself the object of a baffled stare.

'It's the police held me in the Tondo,' Maguire said. O'Malley returned the stare.

'Rodrigo himself, I'm sure of it,' said Maguire. 'I never saw him but he turned up about two o'clock when the shift changed. I heard him through the door. Not what he was saying, but the voice, like a cat lappin' up milk, I'd swear 'twas the Colonel. Byrne's name was mentioned, I heard that, Burke they called him. And yours. He didn't stay, but after he'd gone there was no more cock-fighting.'

'Thanks. 'Tis grand to be kept informed.'

'Sorry, sir.' Maguire stopped himself from adding, 'Thought you knew,' and said, 'It was a while before I grasped it myself. There were no uniforms. Most of the time they were speaking this Filipino.'

He sighed and shut up.

O'Malley said, 'We'd best go.'

He made no move, but gazed through the pink blossoms, nodding his head and scowling. His lips muttered, his fingers fiddled with the threads from which suspended his jacket sleeve. An American car, glittering like a motor show and generously stocked with houseboys, passed along the avenue.

'That's them, sir.'

Unconcerned, concealed by foliage, O'Malley mumbled, 'The Colonel wants us in Manila, staying put. Cruz wants us out. Byrne wants us dead.'

'Beg pardon, sir?'

'Squeezed like a coupla lemons. Thrashin' about like herrin' in a net.'

'Sir?'

'There's a plane at noon. If that woman's to be believed.'

'Woman?'

'What?'

'Sorry, sir. Thought you were saying something.'

'What did Tang say when you phoned?'

'I said you weren't at the hotel, did he happen to know where you might be? He said he didn't but I should try this Senator in Forbes Park. And phone him back.'

'Why'd you phone him anyway?'

'I nearly didn't, 'twas a long shot, but you weren't in the hotel, and when I'd fixed lunch with him he'd kept on about how he'd these friends, he knew everyone. I thought he was toadying, I've known a few like that. He said if we were short of anything, like information, we

must phone him. Those were his words, "short of anything, like information," I remember because I thought
he said "inflammation".'

'We'll do better than phone him, lad. He seems to
know it all. We'll pay him a visit.'

CHAPTER XVIII

LIKE RED INDIANS who have failed in woodcraft, O'Malley and Maguire trod through the copse : trying hard
for silence, but crackling over dead wood, cursing, ques-
tioning the route, stepping on each other's heels, and
emerging startled on the perimeter of terraced lawns
which declined towards a neo-classical mansion in red
brick and white paint. A gardener holding long-handled
shears stared in their direction, then started running
towards the mansion. The Irish *gardai* ran across the
upper lawn and bludgeoned through a hedge into green
gardens whose centrepiece was a circular swimming-
pool.

They could not risk the walkie-talkies and pistols at the
official exits from Forbes Park, and keeping to what
cover the landscape offered they avoided as far as possible the avenues and carborne houseboys. In a relatively
straight line they trekked through private arbours, or-
chards, man-designed glades and dells, and over fences
and walls. Only once were they hailed : a remote shout,
then a dog's barking, which prompted the pair to run
when they had intended to rest for breath. The air was
hot and clammy. Thunder mumbled in the soap-powder
sky, but as if prohibited the storm refused to break over

Forbes Park, adequately green from its batteries of sprin-
klers and hoses, and doing nicely thanks without outside
interference.

The policemen emerged out of clumsy shrubs and
halted, puffing. A stone wall eight feet high, shorn of
ivy and weeds but topped with broken glass, blocked
further progress. O'Malley slung his jacket atop the wall
and said :

'Give me a leg.'

He meant 'Give me a hand,' or hands, for he planted
a shoe in the Sergeant's interlaced fingers and hoisted
himself up.

In the wide and palm-lined road outside Forbes Park
the traffic rolled in the direction, O'Malley assumed, of
Manila. Beyond the road, bordering paddy fields, stood
huddled shacks, and a hut with the sign, Express Laundry. On the pavement below, a gathering of children in
gaudy outfits looked up at him.

'*Vamos*,' O'Malley told them hopefully.

The children started to nudge each other, giggling
and pointing up.

He arranged the ruined jacket under him and
straddled the wall. Reaching down he gripped Maguire's
forearm, then dropped to the pavement as his assistant
hauled himself on to the jacket.

Maguire dropped beside him. Blood from a gash in
the Sergeant's hand splashed to the pavement. From the
jacket came a hearty rending sound as O'Malley tugged
it from the wall.

'Clear off,' he told the giggling and stationary children.

Further along the pavement two teenage girls with
open, fluttering fans had stopped to stare. O'Malley
stared back, reassuring himself that he did not recognize

them. Anyone we recognize now, he thought, police, houseboys, anyone at all, and likely a few hundreds we don't recognize, they're all after us.

The policemen walked fast, Maguire binding a handkerchief round his dripping hand, O'Malley carrying the ailing jacket. Where the traffic slowed for a stop-light they broke into a run, across the road and between cars and buses, hunting for a taxi. One they spotted and waved at drove on, unregarding. A grinning face called to them from a car window. O'Malley did not look to see whether he recognized the face or not.

They walked and ran, and at the next intersection, the traffic immobile at lights, Maguire found a cab with tyres as smooth as glass. O'Malley grabbed a newspaper from a child footpad shouting his wares from car to car, rewarded him with a sprinkling of unknown coins, and joined the Sergeant in the cab's back seat.

'Bel Air,' Maguire was telling the driver, reading from a visiting-card. 'Four, Garcia Avenue, Bel Air.'

O'Malley gazed through the window in quest of an urchin brother of the footpad who might be peddling nuts or pineapples. He was pouring sweat, and though his cold seemed to be improving as swiftly as it had struck, he felt in poor shape; mainly, he supposed, through malnutrition. Apart from an olive, soup and a bread roll, he had eaten nothing since breakfast the previous day. He'd not had the breakfast either, come to think of it. He seemed to have been living off wine and beer.

The car squealed forward on glassy tyres.

CLARK ARMS RAID FOILED – FOURTEEN DEAD, proclaimed the splash in the *Manila Chronicle*.

Before he could read further, O'Malley noticed a familiar face smiling at him from a lesser story alongside, and the heading: 'JUSTICE FOR ALL'. SENATOR CRUZ SPEAKS OUT.

Before studying what the Senator had spoken out about, the Superintendent's wandering eye lighted on a less familiar but still recognizable downpage face under the heading: HILTON MANAGER BRUTALLY MURDERED.

And before allowing his eyes to rove further, or read the smaller print under what they already had seen, O'Malley closed them, and tilted his head against the back of the seat.

He breathed deeply, therapeutically. The sensible course would be the noon flight, or the first flight whatever the hour. He had his passport, return ticket, and if the Sergeant had his too there'd be no need even to return to the Hilton. No one would blame them. More likely they'd be blamed if they stayed a minute longer, considering. Not that it'd much matter being blamed when you were dead, which seemed to be the likely outcome of staying. Brutally murdered, as the papers put it. An honourable, lengthening tradition. A pianist, a Yankee recreation officer, an Aussie hotel manager, fourteen in an arms raid. Not so much as a sniff of Paddy Byrne. Was Byrne away out of it, humming his tiddlye-aye-tye-tyes along the pavements of Buenos Aires or Cape Town? It was a comical class of a country, the Philippines. If you liked your comedy on the sour side.

If they drew a blank with Tang, if Tang was out to policemen, or off raiding arms, or brutally murdered, what then? The Miami Club again, and back to the beginning, though this time without the renegade Col-

onel? Beard her consulship in her investment chambers?
Or break new ground? Major Saunders at Camp Hay,
the salubrious piny resort? Or the other Hilton manager
fella, whatever his name was, Scott, Bob Scott was it?
There'd been no fresh visiting-cards for quite a while,
he'd had none from Lieutenant Ball, or Cruz. But for
how long would he be breaking new ground, with the
noble Senator passing the word round about the two
Mick coppers, and Colonel Rodrigo amusing himself
with his kidnapping games, and the mad noose tighten-
ing all round, and the Maoist lads hopping down from
the hills, and wet weather ahead by the sound and feel
of it? The only course for your reasonable, reasoning
man was Paddy Byrne's course, assuming Byrne had
taken it, which was out. Away. Fast.

Pity this was the one course he and the Sergeant
couldn't take, being not reasonable, reasoning men, not
in a crunch like this, but coppers.

O'Malley said: 'Read that,' and jabbing a finger on
the deceased hotel manager's nose, he shifted the newspaper into a sharing position.

The mutilated body of Mr Bruce Diamond, popular
manager of the Manila Hilton, was recovered last
night from an allotment off Pasig Boulevard. He had
been shot at close range in the head and neck, and his
right hand had been hacked off and removed from the
scene.

Ramon Villadores, 61, married, farmer, who found
the body, has been arrested and is expected to make a
confession today.

Said Capt. H. Taverna, Manila Police: 'We are
holding Villadores as an accessory. This is a political

killing, another cowardly act by the so-called Free
Maoist Liberation Army, and we shall not rest until all
the instigators are brought to book.'

Taverna is confident of further arrests today. The
burly lawman declined to confirm or deny that the
hand of Mr Diamond had been delivered into police
possession independently, prior to the discovery of the
body.

The murder weapon is believed to have been the
popular Smith and Wesson Model 10.

Mr Bob Scott, of Los Angeles, California, assistant
manager of the Manila Hilton, said : 'Naturally we
are all shocked. Bruce was an exceptional person. We
cannot understand how anyone can have done a thing
like this.'

Suspicions were aroused when Mr Diamond failed
to check in at International Airport for a PAL flight
to Tokyo. Reason for the trip was described as 'routine business'.

Marie, Mr Diamond's blonde, vivacious wife, is
expected to fly to Sydney, Australia, with the body
either today or tomorrow. Last night she was with
friends and under heavy sedation.

(Pictures, obituary, p. 11)

'Why?' said Maguire.

'We talked to him, that's why. Same as we talked to
the pianist, and I talked to an American called Ball,
though Ball had to be killed anyway, because you don't
try to blow up Paddy Byrne and expect to go jigging on
your merry way. Not when Byrne can whistle up Cruz
and his private army quick as y'can say knife.'

Maguire, lost, picked at his bristly chin. 'If it's harass-

ment to stop us asking around and finding Byrne, I'd say
it was awful drastic.'

'It's a drastic country, lad. Fourteen dead trying to
get into Clark armoury, all guerrillas. Double that to
include your Yanks and government and I fancy you'd
be nearer the truth.'

They read the splash, then about the curfew-defying
night rally in Luneta Park where Senator Cruz had
called for the release of political prisoners. The Sergeant,
at the time, had been a prisoner in a Tondo cupboard,
the Superintendent had been in the bed of the Irish
honorary consul. Fifty demonstrators had been arrested,
but not, evidently, the eminent Senator. According to
other front page stories, the Army had won a crushing
victory in the central highlands, curfew hours in Manila
were to be rigorously enforced, and extended from 6
p.m. to 6 a.m., and in the province of Mindanao government aircraft had bombed communist strongholds.

O'Malley told the Sergeant about Lieutenant Ball,
and his encounter with the noble Senator. He glossed
over his experiences at the house in Flame Tree Road,
leaving Maguire with the impression that the lady consul
almost, though not exactly, at one point, fleetingly had
come close to, she'd seemed to have it in mind to, she'd
been on the brink of, making an improper proposal.
Through the car window, at the roadside, a scrawny goat
watched the traffic. Outside a bamboo café squatted a
circle of men, spinning a coin.

O'Malley said : 'I was never a great one for guessing,
but if you'd like one to be going on with I'd say the
trouble with the phone lines to Dublin is Colonel Rodrigo.'

Maguire murmured politely. He was wondering whether his hand ought to have a stitch. The pulse beat in the cut.

'Nothing to do with Cruz,' O'Malley said. 'All he cares about is we give up seeking Byrne and go home. There's no problem getting through to Dublin so long as your name's not O'Malley. Remember the cable I sent when we arrived, and the reply sayin' to stay put?'

'I do.'

'Well I'm guessing my cable never got further than police headquarters, and the reply was invented by the Colonel. I'm guessing he put the word in, and all communications between O'Malley and Dublin were locked up till further notice.' O'Malley sponged his brow with a handkerchief more black than white. 'No sense him risking us getting instructions to forget Byrne and come home, don't y'see? And as an additional insurance, just to be certain I don't quit, he has you disappear.'

'So why change his mind and let me walk out? We can quit now.' Maguire adjusted his own grimy handkerchief round his throbbing hand. 'I told you he was mad.'

'You told me he was a ponce. He's very smart and scared as a rabbit, and so'd you be, lad, with this President on your back, screaming about Hart and his rebels, and watching 'em get guns through this singing Irishman who's no sooner gaoled than he's out again, free as y'like. Why you were let out I don't know, but you were going to be out sooner or later, maybe the Colonel couldn't spare the men. Or he changed his mind and decided I'd not a cat's chance of finding Byrne anyway.' O'Malley looked through the window. Girls with sunshades, brown-chested youths carrying their shirts. The sun was blurred : a fuzzy, milky circle low in the sky. 'What puzzles me is why the fella should think I'm going to catch Byrne anyway.'

The point did not puzzle Maguire. If the Chief's reputation had gone before him, into Manila, Rodrigo would have had to have been several classes of pessimist not to have hoped for results.

He said : 'Takes an Irishman to catch an Irishman?'

Takes my backside, O'Malley thought. The Colonel had been clutching at straws. A tower of trouble in his in-tray, and to diminish it even by a fraction he was grabbing at anything that happened along, such as two Irish guards. Please God he'd try no more of his nonsense. Bad enough having the Liberal Opposition lying in wait for you without the local police putting their spanner in.

'Number Four?'

'Hm?'

'Four,' the driver repeated, turning and grinning. 'Garcia. Okay?'

O'Malley, blinking, fought his way out of a famished doze. The cab had halted in a tranquil road flanked by palms. Behind the palms stood big orderly houses in pastel pinks and yellows. Maguire, folding the *Chronicle*, looked in the direction of the driver's pointing finger.

'That one?' Maguire said.

'One-way street, I go on, not turn. You cross road, okay?'

'Where the car is?'

The parked Toyota outside Number Four was already beginning to move in anticipation of two men in obliga-

tory open-neck shirts running from the house. A splash
of white shirt behind the steering-wheel was all that
could be seen of the driver. A third man, not pausing to
close the front door, and dashing in the wake of the
first two, sprinted to catch the accelerating car. Co-
operative arms reached from the rear door and hauled
him inside.

Fuming, cursing, O'Malley dug for pesos for the cab
driver. Maguire scribbled the Toyota's licence number
along the edge of the *Chronicle*. Struggling into his
jacket, O'Malley saw that the hanging sleeve was hanging no longer, but was gone entirely, spirited away and
deposited somewhere in the Manila landscape.

The departing car had departed from sight before
either policeman had alighted from the cab.

CHAPTER XIX

ON HIS BACK, half in the hall, half in an airy library,
was a spreadeagled Filipino with blank eyes and his
throat freshly cut. His lightweight jacket lay open, re-
vealing an empty shoulder-holster.

'*Sic semper* friends and bodyguards,' murmured the
Sergeant, and wondered whether he meant *sic semper* or
semper tyrannis.

'What?' O'Malley said. 'Shut that door, we don't
want the whole neighbourhood in.'

Striding past the bodyguard, he progressed fast and
methodically round the hall, looking into living-rooms, a
kitchen the length of a liner's galley, a mahogany-floored
study. Confirmation that his cold was mending was the

scent of herbs and joss that filtered into his nostrils.
From someyhere above sounded a muffled whine of pop
music.

Don' be afraid . . .

O'Malley and the Sergeant bounded up the stairs,
their feet soundless on the wool carpet. Aiming for the
din, they entered a room furnished with piano, music
stands, a propped double-bass, a dozen chairs, sagging
shelves of records, and stereo hammering out an ancient
Beatles number. Tang sat uncomfortably against the far
wall with his bald moon head askew, as though over-
come by the music's passion. His throat too had been cut.
He wore pyjamas and a dressing-gown awash with
blood.

'Shut that damn racket off,' O'Malley said.

He stood in the middle of the music-room and turned
in a circle, searching for signs, portents, last messages.
The house fell silent as the Sergeant switched off the
record-player. On the piano rested volumes of music
which O'Malley fingered through : Vivaldi, Scarlatti,
Bach. Swallowing, breathing through his mouth, he felt
in Tang's dressing-gown pockets and found Kleenex and
a box of matches.

'Don't just stand, lad. Find the phone.'

'Sir.' Hesitating, Maguire just stood. 'Who're we phoning? The Colonel?'

'It doesn't have to be person-to-person for God's sake.'
O'Malley had taken the record off the turntable and was
perusing the label like a disc-jockey. 'Dial nine-nine-nine
or whatever, just say Tang's dead and give 'em the car's

registration. Hold on a minute. Were the Beatles ever here?'

'Sir?'

'The Beatles. Here in the Philippines. They were your generation, weren't they?'

'Wasn't it in Manila they got roughed up? At the airport?'

'That's what I'm askin'.' O'Malley stood at the shelves, picking through cassettes and records. 'Here, have a look through this lot. Start that end. God, there must be a thousand.'

'Is it the Beatles we're after?'

'No. I don't know. Anything. How'd I know? Who roughed them up, then?'

'The police, wasn't it, and airport officials?' The Sergeant looked at trumpets embellishing the sleeve of Handel's *Messiah*. 'Far as I remember, the President invited them to the Palace and they didn't show up. Said they'd never been invited. Or was it the President's wife? That was it, and she was mortally offended. Ten, twelve years ago.' The fingers of Maguire's good hand prised from the shelf, then returned, *Otello, Faust, Cosi Fan Tutte*. 'All classical up this end, sir.'

'Here too,' O'Malley said, and, stooping, he discovered on the lowest shelf, flat and disarranged, a dozen non-classical : ageing selections from Edith Piaf, Dietrich, Jolson, Noel Coward, Bob Dylan. They comprised about two per cent of the record collection; gifts perhaps, or conversation points for dinner parties. Nothing Irish. The sleeve of *Swingin' Singin'*, the record which had been playing, had only the one Beatles track in a mishmash of dimly-remembered money-spinners of the sixties.

A violent cracking noise, as though somewhere a plank had been bent and split, shook the window-frames and left in the music-room a tremulous hum from the double-bass. The policemen looked at one another, out of the window, at sodden Tang, again at each other.

'I suppose,' O'Malley said, 'that's thunder.'

'Must be,' agreed Maguire, frowning.

Or high explosive, thought O'Malley. A more distant rumbling broke out.

'Get phoning and we'll be away out of it. He'll have one in his bedroom. I don't know what he might have told us but he'll not be tellin' us now.'

Maguire walked from the music-room, opened the first door on his left, and looked into the muzzle of a heavy Webley revolver pointed waveringly at his eyes.

Whether the gun or its wavering was the more frightening, or the paralytic fear of the woman holding the gun, Maguire could not have said, but he found himself incapable of moving. She was seated on a hearthrug with her back against a fluted column of a false fire-place, the shaking pistol held two-handed in her lap.

Mrs Tang? A housekeeper? Even as the Sergeant opened his mouth to try to speak, soothingly, the woman's finger whitened round the trigger and the hammer cocked back.

'Please,' Maguire said, and suddenly he felt detached, uninvolved, as though whatever had to be, had to be, and there was nothing to be done, 'I have to phone. I'm phoning the police.'

'I have phoned them.'

'Would you put that thing away, please?'

'Are you Maguire?'

Maguire wanted to call out to the Chief, but though

the most fraught moments of danger seemed to have passed with the beginning of talk, the gun still pointed, the hands trembled. He deduced she had been dressing when the assassins broke in. She wore a slip and a crêpe skirt patterned with hoops, but she had not progressed so far as shoes, or the green blouse awry on the rumpled bed.

'Wouldn't you let me take it?' he said, but chose not to reach out his hand, or move so much as a centimetre, yet.

'I phoned them,' she said in a dead voice.

'I know. Grand. You did right. How long ago?'

'Five minutes.'

Five minutes invariably meant somewhere between two minutes and ten. Either when the killers had run for their car, five minutes ago; or nine or ten minutes ago when they'd presumably arrived. Killing a bodyguard and a cement manufacturer, Maguire estimated, wouldn't have needed more than a couple of minutes, not if you were professional. Probably Tang had heard something, perhaps the feller in the hall had given a shout, and he'd made the woman stay in the bedroom while he left it. But why'd he gone into the music-room to be killed?

Thunder crackled. Through the window the hot sky was a milky-grey, refusing to rain. The crackling petered away and was replaced, distantly, by chattering that indisputably was machine-gun fire. The thumps were either bombs or field artillery. Maguire felt a presence at his back, and the Super was stepping past him into the bedroom.

' 'Tis too late for guns, they'll do ye no good at all,' O'Malley told the woman, and he took the pistol from her. 'Were you hoping to warn him then? Or were you some sort of bait?'

'Bait?' she echoed, uncomprehending. She had delivered up the gun without protest, seemingly unaware of it. She sat round-shouldered against the fireplace, immobile.

'Keeping him warm and safe till your brother's butlers arrived with their kitchen knives and added him to their list because he knew too much and talked too much.' Finding a cocked revolver in his hand, O'Malley handed it with distaste to the Sergeant. 'This is the Irish honorary consul,' he told Maguire. 'Sister of Senator Cruz, and part-time begetter of revolutions, like the one sounds to be getting steam up right now.'

He went to the window and looked down. A car parked outside the house opposite, and another further along the street, were being loaded with boxes and suitcases by families working in an argumentative, gesticulating rush. A wind tugged at their light clothing, and was causing the palms to sway. The muted rumble of guns was by now persistent. Sirens wailed from the direction of downtown Manila.

'What bait?' said the puzzled, defeated voice from beside the fireplace. 'I loved him.'

'Tang?' said equally puzzled O'Malley, turning from the window. He blew out his cheeks, embarrassed. 'I'm sorry.'

Maguire too watched the drooping consul. He'd not recognized her, though he'd glimpsed her though azaleas in a Forbes Park garden. That could have been only a couple of hours ago. Less. So she'd not been dressing, she'd been undressing.

'She phoned the police, sir,' she says.

'Your friend made it his business to know what was going on,' O'Malley plugged on. To the bereaved mistress, should he speak of Tang as Tang, or Peter? 'Your friend' had the ring of politic compromise. 'F'rinstance, he was able to tell the police Byrne was blackmailing Lieutenant Ball. Ball had got Byrne the entry to Clark Airbase, and the armoury, but when he wanted to close the dealings and be done with it all, the blackmailing started. True?'

No answer.

'Your brother and Byrne can't have been too thrilled at the cover being lifted off the Lieutenant by Tang — by Peter — wouldn't y'say? So for revenge, and to discourage other informers and meddlers, your friend becomes dead.'

'My brother knew I loved Peter!' She was stirred and angry. 'He would never have harmed him!'

'Your Peter's in the next room with his head half off because he meddled.' Ignoring the inference that if Senator Cruz had not harmed Tang, someone else had, and permanently, O'Malley flogged forwards towards a different goal. 'Why did he not stay with his cement, and you? He was a successful businessman —'

'He was a wretched businessman! He was a joke!'

'He didn't want for a quid or two,' O'Malley said with mounting belligerence. 'Don't be tellin' me he was bankrupt.'

'I am telling you nothing!'

'A house this class, silk suits, a woman like you?'

'Get out!'

'How then? His granny left him a million?'

'Yes, if you like!'

'You're lying, it's you, you kept him.'

'Not true.'

'Why not? It's not the cops, the cops don't pay over the odds to informers.'

'The Americans do!'

'Ah.'

Yes. They might. If the information was right, and heavy investment was at stake, and there were Maoists in the hills, and in the street from the noise of it. Looking through the window at the bending palms, O'Malley took from his pocket the black handkerchief and mopped his hands, back and front. Well, the Americans would be wanting a new man for the Manila station. Give 'em an hour or two, the lines to Washington would be buzzin' like wasps.

'So Byrne sent those men to murder –' and he hesitated before settling for – 'Mr Tang.'

'Brought them.'

'Brought them?' O'Malley exchanged a glace with the Sergeant. 'He was driving?'

'He plays it safely.' Her tone was resigned, disinterested. 'Last night was our last raid on the Clark armoury. A failure. Byrne collected his fee, but he stayed away.'

'You saw him in the car, outside?'

'We both did.'

O'Malley looked down from the window. Cases lashed to the roof-rack, the first refugee limousine was pulling away. Two police cars with blinking roof-lights had turned into the street.

'But you've no notion where he'd be headin'?'

'No.'

'If you had, you'd tell me?'

'Yes.'

O'Malley walked back into the music-room. In doubt whether he was supposed to follow or stand like a sentry over the huddled woman in the slip and skirt, Maguire compromised, standing sentry for thirty seconds, then turning to the door. Before reaching the music-room a wave of pop engulfed him. The Chief was crouched over the record-player, fiddling with the controls, and succeeding only in raising the volume.

'*I'm leaving on a jetplane*!' he shouted at Maguire.

'What?'

' "Leaving on a jetplane"! That's what it's called!'

'I know! 'Tis an oldie!'

'What?'

'Kiss me and say you're mine,' Maguire sang inaccurately, endeavouring to catch up with the music.

'Will ye whisht for God's sake and listen!'

They listened with grave faces to Peter, Paul and Mary. The grave face of Sergeant Maguire, having been barked at, also sulked. O'Malley twiddled, demoting the decibel level.

'The next track's nothing, something about bridges, then it's the Beatles, "Hey, Jude" or something, the one we came in on. How long's a track last?'

'Three minutes?'

'So Tang sees Byrne arrive, and he's just time enough to seek out this "Leaving on a Jetplane" and stick it on the gramophone before they're up the stairs and putting the knife in.'

Haughty, committed to his sulks, Maguire declined to answer. He abandoned the revolver to a chair and concentrated on rewinding his hand-bandage.

'C'mon, lad, we're off to the airport,' O'Malley said, and he was marching from the music-room, across the landing.

'What about the woman?'

'What about her?'

'Are we leaving?' Maguire wanted to know, in pursuit down the stairs.

'We are not. But Byrne is.' If I dreamed it right, O'Malley thought, and if Tang was trying to tell us something. 'Remember Byrne, Sergeant? Paddy Byrne? He's why we're here, remember?'

The khaki policemen who were bent over the body-guard's red corpse pulled out their pistols as O'Malley and Maguire turned into the hall. These guns did not waver, and Maguire was confident that two Irish detectives would have been added to the lengthening list of the dead had not Colonel Rodrigo at the same instant rushed in from the rain, and shouted.

The rain beyond the door boomed and sparkled like a glass wall. Such was its din that not until the door had been slammed could anyone hear himself speak.

CHAPTER XX

'Mr O'Malley. You.'

'Me,' O'Malley agreed. 'And Sergeant Maguire. Thanks for Sergeant Maguire. Thanks very much.'

'You are welcome.' The Colonel took off his cap and shook the rain from it. In the few paces from his car to the front door he had been drenched. He glanced at the body half in, half out of the hall. 'Where is Peter Tang?'

'Upstairs. Dead.'

Obscenities fell from the Police Chief's mouth. He snapped his fingers at policemen, motioning them upstairs. There were a half-dozen policemen in the hall, and more entering, their uniforms sopping, rain glistening on their cheeks.

'Might I ask what you are doing here, señor?'

'Leaving. Byrne's at the airport. You coming?'

'The airport is under attack. I am on my way to the Palace.'

'Well, good luck. Are you going to let me have a car?'

Two more policemen wallowed into the hall and banged the door shut. Faintly from above sounded plaintive music. Someone, like a bridge over something water, was laying him down.

'I am short of cars, señor.' The Colonel's expression as he surveyed the bruised face and one-armed jacket implied that had he fifty cars he would not trust one to the Superintendent.

Mind-reading O'Malley said, 'A few impressions of your country to be taking back home.'

'You think you will reach home?'

'If you and your smart games give us half a chance we might.'

'Please, I shall not hinder you, you are at liberty to try.'

'Past coupla days you've been trying your damndest to stop us.'

'The past couple of days are over. The rebels entered Caloocan at five-thirty this morning. They are at the airport. They are in the outskirts of Quezon with mortars and three personnel-carriers. With respect, we have a new situation.'

Which was why, O'Malley realized, Derry's guards were called off, out of the Tondo. He said, 'What about Byrne?'

'Byrne?' The Colonel gestured with brown, contemptuous hands. 'Have you not grasped that there is fighting in the streets? Ewart Hart is in Manila, señor. There is civil war. The Americans sit tight, but for how long? Who cares about Byrne?'

The two senior policemen regarded each other with hostility.

'Goodbye then,' O'Malley said. 'I imagine the Irish consul will be a bore for ye too, but ye'll find her upstairs.'

If music was still playing it was no longer audible above the drumroll of guns and the storm. Colonel Rodrigo settled the cap over his lacquered hair. He pointed at a wiry policeman with braid round his shoulder and chrome badges on his breast and cap.

'Carlos, drive these gentlemen to the airport.' To O'Malley he said, 'It is none of my concern, but I have the impression neither of you possesses a gun.'

'There's one above,' said Sergeant Maguire.

'It's staying there,' O'Malley said, and he opened the door for Carlos to lead into the deluge.

The windscreen wipers washed hypnotically. Carlos drove without fear or imagination, as though the velocity with which he penetrated the embracing murk might decide, one way or the other, the revolution, and bring out the sun.

O'Malley and Maguire sat in silence in the back seat. Through the side windows the cowering palm trees in Roxas Boulevard were blurs. Beyond them, invisibly

across the bay, lay somewhere Corregidor, and Bataan.
An army truck with yellow headlights roared past, heading for the city, its wheels flinging sheet water over the
police car. Traffic was sparse, but such as existed was
encountered with suddenness in the howling rain. Carlos
veered into the fast lane and pushed the speed up to
seventy. Having taken off his cap and placed it on the
empty seat beside him, he lit one-handed a cigarette. A
travel-fatigued fly, too dopey to care, crawled through
the hairs on his forearm.

He's too short for a policeman, he'd never make the
gardai, Maguire considered. He's probably the shortest
policeman in Manila, which is why the Colonel ponce
picked him as chauffeur. If he doesn't kill himself on the
road, and us, he'll be killed in the fightin' at the airport.
He's expendable.

The Sergeant realized he had left the *Chronicle* with
Byrne's car registration at Tang's house. Probably it
would make no difference. No sense mentioning it. The
Super looked grim enough without complications. Grim
and exhausted.

'You might slow her up just a – ' O'Malley started to
tell Carlos, leaning forward and tapping with his fingers
on an epaulette.

Carlos braked so savagely that the tyres screamed in
the gale and the car slewed across the road. As it began
to spin he wrenched the wheel, but the car spun anyway.
O'Malley believed this had to be it, at last the painful,
futile end, in of all places Manila for the love of God,
in the eye of a hurricane, and he'd caused it. A black
unfocused mass hurtled towards them. The skidding car
slowed, drifted, and came to a halt with its rear fender
against an armoured scout car. Carlos threw open the

door and leaped shouting into the rain.

There were other army vehicles, all stationary, blocking the road. Helmeted soldiers in waterproof capes had converged on Carlos, who shouted and waved his arms. One of the soldiers was shouting back and pointing first in one direction, then another. They quarrelled and spat and showed their white teeth like Italian motorists at a traffic-light, while from the back of the car the spectators from Dublin watched to see who would fire the first shot. A crescendo of engine-roar blotted out the voices, creating from the quarrel at the roadblock a mime of silent mouthings and brandished fists, then a pantomime of ducking, skidding buffoons as the belly of a helicopter, almost low enough to be reached for and touched, passed overhead.

Carlos scrambled back into the driving-seat, banged the door, and switched on the ignition. Having recovered the lighted cigarette from the mat at his feet, he said: 'No road. Trouble. We go South Super Highway, okay.'

The car catapulted away from the unbudging army vehicles, careered across Roxas Boulevard, and accelerated east along Libertad.

'How far this way?' O'Malley said.

Carlos puffed cigarette smoke, found the fast lane. 'We make her quick. No rebels. Maybe.'

Somewhere were rebels. Flashes ignited the sky, guns thumped. The car raced past a tilting shack which the gale was dragging along the roadside. The flimsy bamboo box shifted in jerks as though tugged by ropes, and though it had not yet disintegrated, in a moment it would. In the back of the car the policemen sat in silence.

O'Malley thought : I should've let the lad bring the gun.

After the car had turned on to the South Super Highway, Maguire said, 'That jetplane song, 'tis hard to swallow. Wouldn't it've been simpler to scribble it down?'

'For Byrne's boyos to pick up?'

'Tang could've hidden it.'

'He's tellin' us Byrne's leavin' on a jetplane. By the time anyone'd found this copperplate letter you're having him write out and tuck behind the kitchen clock, the bloody jetplane's gone, and Byrne with it.'

'If the record was a message, why didn't they smash it?'

'How'd they know it was a message any more than they knew Byrne was lighting out on a jetplane?'

'How did Tang know?'

'Holy God I don't know how he knew. It was his job, wasn't it? He was paid to know.'

' 'Twould have been simpler,' grumbled Maguire, 'to have told the consul woman. She could've passed it on.'

'And how's Tang to have known they weren't going rooting through the house beheading everyone they found, women first? Look, lad, you tell me why, on noting these boyos coming into the house, Tang goes into that music-room, sorts through his record collection, and puts on "Leaving on a Jetplane".'

Maguire, doggedly sceptical, but not daring to ask if the Super had perhaps dreamed dreams, started unwinding his bandage.

'Are y'saying,' said O'Malley, 'It's the song he'd most like to die to, "Leavin' on a Jetplane"? Out of all that clutter of great spiritual classics? His top desert island disc?' He rubbed his hand over the steamed window. 'God, what now. This is nowhere at all.'

The car had pulled up on the verge. He could see little through the rain, but what he could see was flat fields. He leaned across Maguire and stared through the opposite window. Fifty yards distant, in another flat field, two or three dim figures were running, and a light twin-engine aircraft burned brightly. At a hundred yards stood the silhouette of a Caravelle jet, and somewhere beyond seemed to be the main source of gunfire. No buildings were to be seen. A filament of tracer bullets bisected the murk.

Carlos said: 'You go now, okay.'

O'Malley and Maguire watched the flashing sky, listened to confused shouting from beyond the Caravelle.

'Can you get us to the terminal building?' said O'Malley.

'That way,' Carlos said, pointing into the diagonal rain. 'You go.'

As his passengers merely sat and stared in the direction of the finger, Carlos started to reverse.

'Wait,' said O'Malley. 'All right.'

He followed the Sergeant out of the car and was instantaneously and comprehensively soaked. The car completed its U-turn and with a valedictory beep of the horn departed along the road whence it had come.

O'Malley and Maguire ran in waterlogged shoes past the burning aircraft. They squelched past the tail of the abandoned Caravelle, meeting no one. The rain blinded, the violence of the wind pushed the policemen sideways and caused them to bump into each other. Maguire found himself thinking, as comparison, of rounding Cape

Horn in a skiff. Or swimming round. O'Malley shouted
to him, slowing for breath, then stopping to gaze around
for a bearing. There was no demarcation between earth
and sky, such was the gloom. Two rapid explosions shud-
dered the ground but illuminated nothing.

They ploughed on, now walking, now running, heads
bent into the storm, Maguire always a yard or two in
advance. Ahead and to their left the grey had been pushed
aside by a pink glow. A new explosion ignited the sky
and made O'Malley stumble and almost fall.

'There's the terminal!' Maguire bawled into the rain.
'What?'

They ran along leaking asphalt, O'Malley straining to
recall whether, if the asphalt were a runway, it led to
the arrivals and departures shacks, or away from them,
and should they continue along it, or cross it? Ahead, a
group of crouching figures sprinted across the runway
and were swallowed by the storm, either ignoring or
ignorant of the panting policemen. O'Malley was aware
of a persistent bellow of jet engines as background to the
spasmodic gunfire. Even now, it seemed, in the smoking
heat of the holocaust, some lunatic pilot was optimistic
for take-off.

At least, thought O'Malley, we'll not be meeting any
jetplanes rushing at us and bowling us over, not in this;
and to contradict, to spite him, a jetplane lifted steeply,
blackening the rain with vapour trails, its roar obliterating the cracking thunder in the sky, its lighted windows
mocking at the bedlam below.

To the left a flash illumined the sprinting, crouching
figures, or some other figures, and a parked Cathay
Pacific airliner which seemed to be their goal. The pink
glow had become identifiably the shell of the contem-

porary terminal building, thrice-sabotaged, now burning again. O'Malley, grunting with breathlessness, realized that his shoes were slapping once more through grass, and he hoped please God the Sergeant knew where he was going. Was Byrne aboard the fleeing jet?

If he was, they could go home. Unless the fleeing plane was also the last, until peace and summer were restored.

If Byrne were still here, or anywhere in the Philippines, they stayed. They carried on looking. Come rebellion, typhoon, Armageddon, fleets of cushioned flights to Dublin or whatever.

Maguire glanced back to be sure his Chief was still with him, and shouted, 'That's it there! We came in here!'

The finger of Carlos had pointed accurately enough. They were running again over hard ground, and in front loomed the hut which gave shelter to ticket-counters, customs men, and the carved water-buffalo. An armoured car with soldiers inside bore down on them, and they halted to let it go by, which it did without slowing. Outside the hut was a turmoil of trucks, cars and airport coaches. Soldiers and civilians were hurrying in and out of a lighted doorway. Sandbagged gun-positions had been set up. The huddled soldiers commanding one of these had erected a multi-coloured beach parasol as umbrella and were smoking cigarettes beneath it. In the lighted doorway leaned a dripping PAL ground hostess, in her hands an army combat helmet, in her eyes a befuddled glaze, as though mystified as to what the helmet was, or how she had come by it.

'Arrivals,' Maguire asked the girl, gulping for breath, 'or departures?'

She looked at him without comprehension. O'Malley had not comprehended either, and with a panted 'Pardon, madam,' he pushed the Sergeant past the girl and followed into the glare of the hall.

The hut was no longer for arrivals or for departures, but served as a combined first-aid post and operations centre. Casualties had been laid out on the counters and benches. At the bar a half-dozen officers in battle fatigues and holding drinks were clustered round a major speaking into a field telephone. Nearly everyone was sopping wet. There was nowhere to sit except the floor. Arrived or hopefully departing passengers had congregated in groups with their baggage, distraught and gabbling to whoever would listen, or tensely calm. By the shelves of water-buffalo stood four patient nuns.

'Find out about flights, flights out, any flights out,' O'Malley told the Sergeant, and steered past a moaning infantryman supine on the customs bench towards a face he recognized.

'Have y'seen Byrne?'

'He was here. He tried to get on the Tokyo plane.' Pause. 'Burke, you mean?'

Captain Taverna, at a Philippines Tours desk with two other Manila police, was filling out a printed form. His paunch bulged over his belt, pushing out the holster at an angle. San Miguel beer bottles stood on the desk in front of the policemen. Taverna regarded O'Malley as though impatient to resume work on the form.

'How long ago?' O'Malley said.

'Fifteen minutes.'

'You didn't try to arrest him?'

An explosion shook the shack. A window folded inwards and smashed to the floor. The lights flickered, a child began to cry.

'Burke is not,' said Taverna, scathing, 'a priority.'

'He bloody well is to me. I want a car.'

'Ask the Army. They aim to shoot Byrne on sight. But they're not going out of their way. They have priorities too.'

'I said I want a car.'

'Hertz desk, to the right.'

'From you, Captain. And a driver.'

'You are crazy.'

'Colonel Rodrigo says I get a car and a driver,' O'Malley lied, and taking the pen from Taverna's fist he pressed its point against the tip of the wide brown nose.

Taverna's eyes swivelled down to the pen, then round to the closer of his two colleagues. 'Drive him.'

O'Malley tossed the pen on to the desk, from where it bounced to the floor, and said, 'You can get on with your expenses.'

He found the Sergeant in conversation with a tea-gulping pilot of Singapore Airlines.

'C'mon, lad, we're going after Byrne.'

'You've found him?'

O'Malley did not reply, but with Maguire and the new driver in tow headed through the shack. Leaders, prophets, captains of industry, often enough they'd all arrived at decisions not from what the computer fed 'em but by guessing, or inspiration, or desperation, or a word from God, and all this a sprig like Derry Maguire might accept. But how could he explain to the Sergeant that he, a flatfoot, was acting on a dream?

CHAPTER XXI

A REEK of sweat and San Miguel carried from the driver to the front passenger-seat where sat O'Malley, and to Maguire in the back. The headlamps flung two cones of light into the storm as the police car accelerated between a petrol tanker and a makeshift gun-emplacement and turned towards the red glow that was the carcass of the terminal building.

Maguire leaned forward and said:

'There's no flights coming in, sir, and all flights out are cancelled, but one to Tokyo got away. Seems they're dashin' out of it if they can. There's one for Singapore been trying to get out for two hours but there's some short-circuit or something in the landing-gear.'

'Where is it, the Singapore one?'

'Think he said Number Three. Number Three runway.'

'Where's Number Three runway?' O'Malley said to the driver.

'Other side the terminal.'

'That terminal?'

'Yes.'

'Far?'

'No. The other side.'

Through slashing windscreen wipers O'Malley watched the fluttering pink and orange of the terminal building draw closer. For the first time in a long time he felt satisfaction. There was meat to the dream. An aircraft by the terminal was waiting to take off. There, already, was half a reason for Paddy Byrne to be in the terminal, or by it, even if only to keep dry, biding his time before running for the plane.

Why would he bide his time?

'You want the terminal or the runway?' the driver said.

'I want the terminal. Sergeant Maguire wants the Singapore plane, if it's there. God above, what class of weather d'ye call this?'

'Typhoon.'

The Superintendent was not surprised. He had begun to wonder whether the car would reach the burning terminal, now only a hundred yards ahead. The road was awash, decorated from place to place with a floating palm tree, a bush, débris. At one point the car churned through water up to its hubcaps. The wind bludgeoned at a hundred miles an hour, and was strengthening. As though one side or the other had gained the advantage, the gunfire seemed less insistent than earlier. But if an aircraft survived the guerrillas, could it take off in a typhoon? If not, Byrne was stranded.

But a Tokyo plane, O'Malley remembered, had taken off.

Only one corner of the terminal was alight. In compensation the corner blazed with a festive incandescence. O'Malley was unable to fathom how bare walls and floors of steel and concrete could blaze at all, especially in this deluge, but they were managing to. The only hint at activity was a solitary, inactive fire appliance, and a clutter of firemen sheltering in its cabin, watching the flames. They had switched their attention from the fire to the police car but were making no attempt to brave the rain with either greetings or warnings. The car halted at the terminal's forlorn entrance. O'Malley gripped the door-handle.

'Derry, you'll have a peek inside that plane that's waiting to take off. If Byrne's there, don't mess with him, come back here. I'll be in the terminal. Come back anyway. Quick as y'like.'

He was startled by a feeling of fellowship with the Sergeant. He wanted to say more, a benediction, and shake the gashed hand, or anyway the good hand. But if the pair of them lived through the next hours to return to Dublin, he'd not want to be hefting mawkish memories around, neither would Maguire, and the two of them extra polite and looking the other way when they met on Dame Street and up and down the steps of the Castle.

'Good luck so,' O'Malley said.

He dashed for the entrance, over the last half-dozen paces treading through wind-flattened bracken and brambles. The fire, burning in the furthest corner of the building, was nowhere in evidence from the gaping, doorless entrance. If it boomed and crackled, the sound was lost in the great bedlam of the typhoon. When he looked round, police car, driver and Maguire were gone.

Staying close to the wall, O'Malley stepped inside the terminal, stood still, and surveyed. The main hall was oblong, vast, bereft of furnishings apart from the rows of counters that were fixtures. If Byrne were here, the two of them might play in-and-out-the-counters for the rest of the morning. And this was but one hall on one floor. If Byrne proposed to curl up in some deeper recess of the building, whether above or below ground level, there'd be need of dogs and twenty men to seek him out.

O'Malley grimaced, resisting as best he could the sense

of defeat which told him he was wasting his time. He concentrated on the immediate geography. Twin escalators stood in the hall's centre, reaching down to no one knew what misbegotten basement territory, and up to a mezzanine. The grey half-light was no less penetrable than outside; indeed, visibility was clearer than in the blanket rain. He could see doors and openings of corridors at either end of the hall, and in front, straight across the hall, the square holes that had been windows. The notice on the wall beside his head read :

Pursuant to Ordinance No. 3820, possessors of firearms and other dangerous weapons . . .

Keeping to the wall, eyes roaming the hall, its counters, what little he could see of the mezzanine above, O'Malley began a circuit. He walked without hurry, a plodding copper's walk, as though enjoying the sea air on a Sunday at Sandymount, or uniformed again, thirty years ago, testing the door-handles in Amiens Street. He could not hear his footfalls for the raging of the rain and wind outside. He was aware he would not be able to hear those of Byrne either.

At the end of the hall he looked into passages and turnings leading to long-abandoned cafeterias, bars, first-aid rooms, children's nurseries. He kept on, past a florist's, a confectioner's, a newsagent's. The plate glass had been smashed, by saboteurs or by vandals, and nothing remained in the shops except broken glass. Through a window in the long wall opposite the entrance he looked out and saw, massive against the sky, a jetplane of Singapore Airlines.

It stood with lighted windows and doorways directly

behind the terminal and not a hundred yards away. Its tail was diagonally towards the building, and flickered pinkly from the glow thrown from the blazing corner. Had the police car approached the terminal from any direction but head-on, he could not have helped but see it before now. Two army trucks were among a dozen vehicles drawn up around the aircraft. A searchlight atop an armoured car turned with a slow circular motion, its beam lighting the gloom. When figures appeared, they were running at full tilt through the storm, from one vehicle to another, or up the steps into the jet-plane. O'Malley tried and failed to identify the police car, and wondered if Derry was yet aboard, perusing faces. Here was one plane, he thought, the army didn't intend the guerrillas to get their hands on.

And if the army had Byrne among its targets for shooting on sight, as Captain Taverna had believed, he'd have to be slippery, brave, and lucky as the jack of trumps to pass through the encircling vehicles.

O'Malley left the wall and walked among the counters. At every step the counters hid or revealed some part of him. The light in the centre of the main hall was very fair. If Byrne wanted to shoot he could do so now.

Would he shoot without first a speech, a boast, a verse of tenor song perhaps, in celebration of him, mother, and the hills of Wicklow? Byrne was a psychopath. O'Malley did not know what the man would do.

He walked half-way down an escalator. Seeing the blackness below, where without a flashlight he would find nothing, he returned to the ground level and walked up the escalator to the mezzanine. Here, were he Byrne, and had watched the arrival of the car and the Dublin Superintendent, he would have hidden: one eye on the stalking copper below, the other at a window, checking the Singapore jetplane and its army guards.

O'Malley walked to a window. To approach close enough to see the jetplane he had to suffer a drenching from the rain which lashed in through the empty frame. He turned away, looked to left, right, and started walking. Shallow mahogany screens had been fitted along the wall to form a succession of alcoves, each with its window, where the architect's leaping imagination had envisaged idle families and businessmen biting on peanuts and enjoying the airport landscape. O'Malley had passed only one alcove when a gun exploded, and he lurched sideways into the angle between screen and wall.

This was the only cover available, and if Byrne could see him it was not even cover. O'Malley could see no one. He pressed himself into the angle, breathing hard, waiting. He had to wait no longer than a count of three. Simultaneously with the second gunshot the mahogany in front of his knees shattered.

The crown of splintered wood pointed inwards, towards the knee. O'Malley, sweating, stared at it. Byrne had to be the other side of the screen, somewhere. The pistol exploded a third time, not with further smashing of wood but with a shrieking ricochet off concrete. O'Malley threw himself prone under the window, and as he started to drag himself forward, away from the screen, the gun fired twice more, blasting the mahogany where O'Malley had stood and sprinkling the back of his head with concrete chips and plaster.

Where to now? O'Malley twisted his head and saw the screen, holed, but still recognizably a screen. He wanted to get up and run, risking exposure for the sake of more substantial shelter. But he knew of no other shelter. There were only alcoves. He lay motionless, stifling with his hand the rasp of his breathing, awaiting the next bullet. If earlier bullets had missed, so might the next.

In competition with the typhoon his grunting breath was inaudible even to himself. The fact did not register. O'Malley held his knuckles between his teeth, waiting.

He heard gunfire, but distantly from a machine-gun. Maybe a mile away.

Prone, waiting, aware he should be praying, instead he counted the bullets fired. Byrne's bullets. Five.

If Byrne came closer, O'Malley reasoned, into the alcove, he himself would risk a bullet, or believed he would. He'd assume the copper had a gun. How long'd he assume if he were not fired at?

How long since Byrne last had fired? Half a minute? A minute? Prone, waiting O'Malley wished he could know how many bullets the gun held. Was Byrne reloading? Did there remain one bullet, then no more? A single remaining bullet would explain the calm.

O'Malley held his fists to his eyes, trying to put himself in Byrne's place. Byrne couldn't know if he'd hit his target or not. But he'd not chance it, he'd assume not, until he knew different. If one bullet remained it would have to count. To count, the copper would have to come into the open. To come into the open he'd have to be spoken to, and drawn out. Cajoled. Tricked. Goaded. Something. Why didn't the fella speak?

An Irish voice, Dublin as the Liffey, called: 'Mr O'Malley! Are yez listenin'?'

'Sir, wait on!' came, from ground level, another Dublin accent. Whatever advice it might have been about to give was lost in the pistol's roar.

O'Malley rolled over, out of the alcove. A dozen paces from him, Byrne in a skyblue raincoat was at the mezzanine balustrade, arm outstretched, gun pointing down into the main hall. Echoes of the explosion clamoured in O'Malley's ears. Struggling to his feet, he saw Maguire looking up from the hall. Not only did the Sergeant not fall, he started to run for the escalator. Byrne's gun followed him, aiming. To O'Malley the gun seemed to aim interminably. Then the arm dropped. Six, thought O'Malley. Then Byrne glanced round at him, and the two men stared at each other.

Byrne's face was suntanned, flabby and bespectacled. The spectacle rims rested on bulges of flesh beneath the eyes, and from under the chin sagged a dewlap of skin. The straggling hair was thin, gone from the temples. O'Malley's image of his quarry, the face in dreams he had dreamed, had been a composite of the scowling thug encountered several years ago in court, and the concert-platform tenor of the old publicity photographs. Here was the reality : middle-aged, podgy, wearing a look of disbelief. Byrne took a step sideways, dropped the gun, grabbed a doeskin travelling-bag and a briefcase, turned, and ran.

O'Malley charged after him, and in O'Malley's wake dashed Maguire. Along the mezzanine, down broad un-carpeted stairs, past closed doors in a corridor, through an open door, and into a hall where one wall was lined with empty beer cans as though in readiness for a contest in marksmanship, and the exterior wall was missing except for a rump of concrete blocks. The typhoon tore through the hall. Byrne, burdened by bags, ran on with the desperation of the damned, and from the manner in which his head turned to left and right, searching, with no better knowledge of the terminal's geography than had his pursuers. The gap separating him from the weary Superintendent had widened to twenty strides, and rounding the hall's rain-washed corner O'Malley skidded and fell. Before he was on his feet again, wondering from the pain in his ankle whether he would be progressing much further, the Sergeant had overtaken him and was pounding after Byrne like a moustached peeler from the era of gaslight and gin at tuppence a tot.

O'Malley hobbled through glass doors which had lost their glass, and for want of an alternative up stone stairs and into thickening smoke. So long as the hurt foot hung free and was not used for walking, the pain in the ankle was bearable. He walked anyway, and tried to run. Higher up banged a door. Either a door, or shooting had broken out again.

Holding with one hand to the iron banister, clamping his black handkerchief to nose and mouth with the other, O'Malley hauled himself upwards, and at the top of the second flight of steps saw that they divided, a choice of left or right for the final assault on the summit. The dozen steps of the left-hand flight ended at a square and horizontal door of frosted glass, like an outsize skylight. The glass stood open, buffeted by the storm, and in O'Malley's view about to slam shut and smash, and shower him with glass. At the head of the right-hand flight the skylight was missing, as were the upper steps, and had been replaced by flames and smoke. O'Malley climbed to the left.

He surfaced, head and shoulders, and looked across a plateau of storm-swept concrete which might have been a roof, or a portion of an unfinished extension, or a floor from which roof and walls had fallen away. Flames curled over its edge. Beyond stood the Singapore Airlines jetplane, and from the same direction came a renewed clatter of shooting. Head bent, drenched and wind-blown once again, O'Malley stepped on to the concrete.

'Get down!' Maguire's voice shouted.

O'Malley supposed the command to be directed at Byrne, whom he spotted to his right, shambling in a crouch along the side of the roof as though searching for a fire-escape or a bridge or a spot from where he might jump. He moved clumsily on bent knees, brief-case and travelling-bag swinging in his hands. Maguire was on all fours, bawling at his Chief.

'Gerron down, sir! They're takin' potshots!'

Whether under orders, nervous, or merely bored, a group of helmeted sharpshooters from the trucks near the jetplane were running forward, halting to take aim and fire at the men on the burning terminal, and again running forward. O'Malley threw himself flat, where he could neither see over the plateau's edge nor be seen. Byrne, he realized, already had been hit.

'Byrne!' Maguire called.

Byrne was hit once more. One at least of the soldiers was a marksman. With a flutter of skyblue raincoat Byrne and his baggage tipped over the edge.

CHAPTER XXII

THE POLICEMEN crawled on their bellies and met close to the smouldering edge of the plateau. They had to shout to be heard above the storm and the jetplane's engine-roar.

'Take heed of the fire, sir. I'll look.'

'Stay where y'are, for Jesus' sake. You'll get your head shot off.'

Disobedient, the Sergeant crawled the last yards with O'Malley. A flame squirted from nowhere, singed his wrist, and vanished. Four storeys below, the sharpshooters were trampling among briars in which was embedded a patch of sky blue. Indifferent now that the score had been made, the target hit, two of the soldiers started trotting back towards the trucks. The pods of the jetplane quivered as the engines revved in a crescendo of sound.

O'Malley was conscious of immense fatigue and anticlimax. The blot of sky blue on the dingy ground below offered neither satisfaction nor even a sense of release. No use pretendin' he'd been a good Catholic, that one, O'Malley thought. He'd been good for nothing only troublemaking. The Sergeant, he realized, was shouting in his ear.

'If we're sharp, sir, we can get off to Singapore, but she'll not wait.'

'Singapore? We've no tickets, lad. We've –'

' 'Tis no matter. There's papers we sign on board.'

'Ye've fixed something?'

'I've tried.'

They crawled back from the edge and across the tidal concrete. Helped by Maguire, the Superintendent lowered himself through the skylight and down stone steps. They progressed along passages, down stairs, lost themselves in looted halls, found the mezzanine, the escalator, and swaying between counters, O'Malley leaning for support against Maguire, met Colonel Rodrigo walking on his burnished tap-dancer's feet through the doorless entrance.

He was accompanied by the lunatic driver Carlos and a tribe of policemen. Forgetting to smile, Manila's Chief of Police said: 'You have found Byrne?'

'Outside at the back,' O'Malley said. 'There'll be money in his bags so you'd best hurry or you'll be late for the distribution. Thought you were off to the Palace.'

'The Palace is evacuated. Our information is that Ewart Hart will endeavour to link with Byrne.'

'That's the new priority, is it?' O'Malley said, and limped past the uniforms and out of the terminal.

Maguire wrapped round his neck the Super's sleeveless arm and together the pair lumbered like a three-legged race through the typhoon. They were fifty yards from the jetplane when they saw the passenger steps up to the forward door being dragged clear. Several of the encircling vehicles were driving to a safer distance. O'Malley wanted to tell the Sergeant he could stop trying now, they were too late, but the pain in his ankle preoccupied him, and he let Maguire get on with it. He wondered if the Filipino soldier who loomed with outstretched arm intended to execute them on the spot.

But there was no pistol in his hand. The hand was shaking the Sergeant's hand, gash as well, as though the two were mates from schooldays. The soldier turned and shouted, waved an arm, and the steps were rolled up to the aircraft. Someone must have been watching through a window because before the policemen were half-way up the steps the door into the Douglas DC8 of Singapore Airlines opened.

'How much,' panted O'Malley, climbing, 'you pay your pal?'

'What I had,' panted Maguire. 'About twelve quid. Will I get it back?'

'Ye will sure. Write it down.'

'Thanks. He's a brigadier.'

'They've a fine plethora of brigadiers in the Philippines Army. 'Tis the politics. I read it in that book y'had, whatever it was.'

'*Islands in Ferment*. Will it be all right to claim for that too?'

'And your sister's sash. That sash you were done for. Write it all down.'

A lissom Malay hostess in a sarong promised O'Malley and Maguire that she'd do her best to find dry clothes for them, but until take-off would they keep their seatbelts fastened please. The plane taxied, its pace quickened, then slowed, and the aircraft came to a stop. Smiling, in spite of everything, like the Queen of the Night, the hostess trod fast along the aisle. Word of a minor electrical fault was bandied among the passengers.

For twenty minutes the Dublin detectives sat like sodden brigands in a gathering suspense. The aircraft was no more than a quarter full, but those who had found their way aboard generated an air of queasy trepidation. Would the minor fault develop into a major fault?

Would lightning, or a grenade, strike the plane? Rain gusted into the cabin as the forward door opened, then closed, having admitted Colonel Rodrigo.

'Mother of God, what now?' O'Malley murmured.

The Colonel advanced along the aisle like a lover unable, even at the irrevocable moment of parting, to leave the loved one alone. Under the liquorice eyebrows the eyes searched and found the Irish detectives. He progressed towards them. In his hand he carried a cylindrical *Chronicle*-wrapped package, like fish and chips.

'Maybe,' he said, looking down from the aisle, 'you would be interested, Senator Cruz is reported in occupation of the Palace.'

'Oh yes?' O'Malley said.

'Possibly it is a rumour.'

'You get rumours, time like this.'

'Such occupation would be premature. The army has remained loyal, on the whole.'

'Good, good.'

The Colonel looked from O'Malley to silent Maguire, and back to O'Malley. He seemed about to speak, to offer further intelligence on the insurrection, but changed his mind, and shrugged. A whiff of pomade wafted to the Irish policemen. He held out the package. The underside was a damp and grubby russet colour.

'For you, for your records. I was thinking of identification. You may be glad of the prints.'

The Superintendent and the Sergeant regarded the offered package. Finally, O'Malley gestured above his head.

'P'raps you'd leave it in the locker.'

The Colonel placed the package in the overhead locker.

'Adios, gentlemen.'

'Adios,' said O'Malley.

' 'Bye,' Maguire said.

Through the window the policemen watched the Colonel tread smartly down the steps which had been towed for him along the runway. Captain Taverna jumped from a waiting police car and opened the door.

The Queen of the Night passed smiling along the aisle, bestowing sweetness and personal attention on the scattered passengers, apologizing that there would be little to eat due to the flight being unscheduled and unprepared. A few biscuits. Some curried eggs. But there would be bar service. After take-off.

'Biscuits, curried eggs and bar service,' echoed O'Malley, and he wanted to reach across the Sergeant and shake the hand of the hostess. 'D'ye know, will we be havin' a filum at all?'

The jetplane moved, gathered speed, and took off like a rocket into the typhoon.